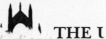

A dull murmur, like distant THE U *reached their ears and brought Biggles to his feet with a rush. 'What is it?' he gasped.*

At the first sound Dickpa had leapt for the flashlight. 'Quick,' he snapped, as the floor of the cave sagged sickeningly. 'Get out — it's an earthquake! Ah — stop!' he screamed.

There came a definite roar from somewhere down the tunnel up which they had come, and the air was filled with a cloud of choking, blinding dust. The sides of the cave quivered like jelly, and a few pieces of rock fell from the roof with a crash; then all was still again.

Captain W. E. Johns was born in Hertfordshire in 1893. He flew with the Royal Flying Corps in the First World War and made a daring escape from a German prison camp in 1918. Between the wars he edited *Flying* and *Popular Flying* and became a writer for the Ministry of Defence. The first Biggles story, *Biggles the Camels are Coming* was published in 1932, and W. E. Johns went on to write a staggering 102 Biggles titles before his death in 1968.

kidsatrandomhouse.co.uk

BIGGLES BOOKS
PUBLISHED IN THIS EDITION

FIRST WORLD WAR:
Biggles Learns to Fly
Biggles Flies East
Biggles the Camels are Coming
Biggles of the Fighter Squadron
Biggles in France
Biggles and the Rescue Flight

BETWEEN THE WARS:
Biggles and the Cruise of the Condor
Biggles and Co.
Biggles Flies West
Biggles Goes to War
Biggles and the Black Peril
Biggles in Spain

SECOND WORLD WAR:
Biggles Defies the Swastika
Biggles Delivers the Goods
Biggles Defends the Desert
Biggles Fails to Return

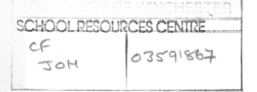

BIGGLES
AND THE
THE CRUISE *of the*
CONDOR

CAPTAIN W.E. JOHNS

RED FOX

Red Fox would like to express their grateful thanks
for help given in the preparation of these editions to Jennifer Schofield,
author of *By Jove, Biggles*, Linda Shaughnessy of A. P. Watt Ltd
and especially to the late John Trendler.

BIGGLES AND THE CRUISE OF THE CONDOR
A RED FOX BOOK 9780099938705

First published in Great Britain as The Cruise of the Condor: a Biggles
Story by John Hamilton, 1933

This Red Fox edition published 2004

8

The Random House Group Limited supports The Forest Stewardship
Council (FSC), the leading international forest certification organisation.
All our titles that are printed on Greenpeace approved FSC certified paper
carry the FSC logo. Our paper procurement policy can be found at:
www.rbooks.co.uk/environment.

Red Fox Books are published by Random House Children's Books,
61–63 Uxbridge Road, London W5 5SA,
A Random House Group Company

Addresses for companies within The Random House Group Limited
can be found at:
www.randomhouse.co.uk/offices.ht

THE RANDOM HOUSE GROUP Limited Reg. No. 954009

A CIP catalogue record for this book is available from the British Library.

Printed and bound in Great Britain by
CPI Antony Rowe, Chippenham, Wiltshire

Contents

The word 'Hun' used in this book was the generic term for anything belonging to the German enemy. It was used in a familiar sense, rather than derogatory. Witness the fact that in the R.F.C. a hun was also a pupil at a flying training school.

W.E.J.

Chapter 1
Biggles Gets A Shock

'The trouble about civil life is that nothing ever seems to happen. What interest people got out of it before the War I can't imagine; it must have been deadly dull. Even peace-time flying is so tame that I can't get a kick out of it. No Archie,* no Huns,** no nothing — just fly from here to there, and there you are. This peace seems a grim business to me; what do you think about it?'

The speaker paused and glanced moodily at his companion, as if seeking confirmation of these unusual sentiments. Slim, clean shaven, and as straight as a lance, his carriage suggested military training that was half denied by the odd, wistful look on his pale, rather boyish face; tiny lines graven around the corners of his mouth and steady grey eyes gave him an expression of self-confidence and assurance beyond his years. His voice was crisp and decisive, and carried a hidden note of authority, as in one accustomed to making decisions and being obeyed.

His companion was about the same age, perhaps a trifle younger, but rather more stocky in build. His round, freckled face, surmounted by an untidy crop of fair hair, carried eyes that twinkled humorously at the slightest pretext. There was little about either of them to show that they had been two of the most brilliant

* RAF slang for anti-aircraft fire.
** Slang term for Germans or anything German.

7

air fighters in the War, a pair who, towards the end of 1918, were known on the British side of the lines of the Western Front* as nearly invincible, and on the German side as a combination to be avoided.

The speaker was, in fact, Major James Bigglesworth, D.S.O., M.C.,** popularly known as Biggles, who in October 1918 had commanded No. 266 Squadron in France. Victor of thirty-five confirmed combats and many others unclaimed, he was known, at least by reputation, from Belgium to the Swiss frontier.

The other was his close friend and comrade-at-arms, Captain Algernon Lacey, more often simply known as Algy, who had finished the War as a flight commander in the same squadron, with twenty victories signed up in his log-book.

'I agree,' he replied morosely, in answer to Biggles's complaint; 'but what can we do about it? Nothing! I expect we shall get used to it in time.'

'I shall pass out with boredom in the meantime,' replied Biggles with conviction, 'that's why I suggested coming down here to see Dickpa. He should be able to shoot us a good yarn or two.'

'Why on earth do you call your uncle Dickpa?'

Biggles laughed. 'I don't know,' he replied. 'I used to call my guvnor*** "Pa" when I was a toddler, and when his brother Dick came down to see him I just naturally called him Dickpa. I've never called him anything else. I haven't seen him for years, because, as I told you, he's an explorer and is very seldom in this country. Hearing he was back on one of his rare visits, I thought I'd slip along and see the old chap

---

* The Front line trenches of World War I stretching from the North Sea to the Swiss frontier.
** Distinguished Service Order, Military Cross (two medals).
*** Slang: father.

while I had the chance, and I thought you'd like to come along too. He's got an interesting collection of stuff from all sorts of out-of-the-world places. There's the house now, straight ahead.'

They walked slowly on down the leafy drive towards an old, red-bricked Elizabethan house, which they could now see through the trees, in silence, for it was midsummer and the sun was hot.

'Well, there are times when I positively ache to hear a gun go off,' went on Biggles presently. 'Sheer habit, of course—'

'Stick 'em up!'

Biggles stopped dead and stared, in wide-eyed amazement, in the direction from which the words had come. Algy also stopped, blinked, and shook his head like a prize-fighter who had just intercepted a straight left to the point of the jaw.

'Looks as if my dreams are coming true,' muttered Biggles softly. 'Can you see what I see, Algy, or shall I wake up in a minute?'

'Quit squarkin' and do as you're told,' growled a coarse nasal voice with a pungent American accent. The speaker, a tall, sun-burned man with a squint and a skin that had at some time been ravaged by smallpox, took a pace forward to emphasize his words. In his hand, held low on his hip, was a squat, wicked-looking automatic. 'You heard me,' he went on, scowling evilly.

'Yes, I heard you,' replied Biggles evenly, eyeing the speaker with interest, 'but aren't you making a mistake? This is England, my friend, not America; and we have our own way of dealing with gun-thugs, as you'll presently learn, I hope. If it's money you want, you've made a boob, because I haven't any.'

'Say, are you telling me?' snarled the man. 'Step

back the way you came, pronto; you're not wanted here.'

Biggles looked at the American coldly and sat down on the stone wall that bordered the drive. 'Let's discuss this sensibly,' he said gently; and Algy who had heard that tone of voice before, quivered instinctively in anticipation of the action he knew was coming.

'Talk nothing. On your feet, baby, and step out!'

Biggles sighed wearily. 'Well, you seem to have—what do you call it?—the low-down on us,' he muttered. 'Come on, Algy, let's go. There's a present for you,' he added as an afterthought to their aggressor, and with his left hand flicked a pebble high into the air above the man's head.

It was an old, old trick, but, like many old tricks, it came off. The man's eyes instinctively lifted to watch the flight of the pebble, and he side-stepped to let it fall. But, even as his eyes lifted, Biggles's right hand shot out and hurled a large, jagged piece of stone, that he had taken from the wall, straight at the man's head. It was a good shot, and took him fairly and squarely between the eyes. Biggles, his fists clenched, seemed to follow the stone in its flight across the drive, but he pulled up dead, with a muttered exclamation of disgust, for the man, moaning feebly, lay in a semi-conscious heap at his feet. The automatic had fallen from his nerveless fingers, and Biggles, with a quick movement, picked it up and dropped it in his own pocket.

'Great jumping cats, I hope you haven't killed him!' gasped Algy, hurrying across and looking aghast at the trickle of blood that was flowing from a jagged wound in the man's forehead.

'Killed nothing!' sneered Biggles impatiently, white with anger. 'What of it, anyway? Do you think that, after being shot at abroad for years, I'm going to have people making a dart-board of me in my own country? Not on your life. If, after spending my precious youth fighting the King's* enemies, I can't fight one of my own, it's a pity. I don't understand what it's all about, though; there's something wrong here. I hope Dickpa is all right; come on, let's get along.' And, without another glance at their fallen foe, he strode off quickly up the drive.

With Algy at his heels, he reached the front door and jangled the great old-fashioned bell noisily. There was no reply. Again he pulled the chain. 'Anyone at home here?' he shouted in a loud voice.

The squeaking of a lattice window above them made them glance upwards, and the sight that met their eyes brought another shout from Biggles. Pointing down at them were the twin muzzles of a 12-bore sporting gun. Behind them, half hidden in shadow, they could just discern a face, the lower half of which was buried in a grey beard.

'Hi! Don't shoot! It's me, Dickpa!' yelled Biggles, ducking.

'Throw yourself flat; you're liable to be shot!' cried Dickpa quickly. 'I'm coming down.' The window slammed shut as Biggles flung himself at full length on the gravel path, with Algy beside him.

'When Dickpa says lie down, I lie down. He's no fool, believe me,' muttered Biggles anxiously.

Algy grinned. 'Picture of two young gentlemen visiting uncle in the country,' he chuckled. 'I've been thrown out on my ear before today, but I believe this is the first time I've gone in on it. If this is how you visit your uncles, you might have warned me to bring some overalls. This is my best suit—'

* King George V 1910–1935.

11

The rattle of chains and the withdrawing of bolts inside the door cut him short. The great iron-studded oak portal swung open a few inches and a pair of deep-set eyes peered through the crack at them. 'Quick, jump for it!' cried Dickpa, and flung the door wide open.

Together the two airmen leapt across the threshold, and as the door slammed behind them they heard a sharp report from somewhere outside and the dull thud of a striking bullet. Algy, who had landed on a loose bearskin rug, skidded violently, and, after making a wild effort to save himself, measured his length on the floor.

'Can't you land without stunting?' grinned Biggles.

Algy groaned. 'Is this how you usually visit your uncles?' he snarled, picking himself up and rubbing his knee ruefully.

But Biggles had turned to the elderly man, who was bolting the door securely. 'What's going on, Dickpa?' he cried in astonishment. 'Have you turned this place into a madhouse? Never mind your knee, Algy; meet Dickpa—Dickpa, meet Algy—the man who managed to survive the War more by luck than judgement.'

Algy glanced up and found himself looking into a rugged, weather-beaten face, in which a pair of rather mild blue eyes twinkled brightly. 'Pleased to meet you, sir,' he said. 'We seem to have arrived at an entertaining moment.'

'You couldn't have arrived at a better time,' replied the old traveller quickly. 'I'm badly in need of reinforcements. There are some gentlemen outside who—'

'Hold people up at the revolver-point,' broke in Biggles.

'How do you know?'

'One of 'em tried it on us.'

'The rascal! What did you do?'

'Smote him between the eyes with half a brick.'

'Splendid! cried the old man enthusiastically. 'I hope he liked it. But you must be hungry. Come and have some food and I'll tell you all about it.

'You are going to find it hard to believe the story I am about to tell you,' went on Dickpa when they had pulled up their chairs in the old, oak-panelled dining-room to a rather frugal meal of cold beef and pickles. 'In the first place, you had better understand I am in a state of siege.'

Biggles nearly swallowed a pickled onion in trying to speak. 'Siege?' he managed to gasp. 'Who—'

'Wait a moment; don't be so impatient,' interrupted Dickpa. 'I trust it will not be necessary to use them, but I have taken the precaution of bringing in from the gun-room what weapons I have available. From time to time I let drive from one of the windows with that elephant gun on the left, in order to encourage the enemy to keep at a distance.'

The two airmen followed his eyes to the wall, against which leaned a row of gleaming metal barrels—a Sharp's Express rifle, a couple of 12-bores, a .410 collector's gun, and an elephant gun, beside which a .22 rifle looked ridiculously out of place.

'But why on earth don't you ring up the police?' cried Biggles in amazement.

'Because it wouldn't be the slightest use,' replied Dickpa gravely. 'They've cut the telephone wires, anyway. But I'll tell you the story if you'll listen.'

'Go ahead, Dickpa. I won't interrupt,' said Biggles apologetically.

The old explorer filled a well-worn briar pipe, and

when he had got it going to his satisfaction he continued.

'The story really begins some years ago. As you know, I've spent my life exploring out-of-the-way parts of the world, but chiefly in South America. I have long held the opinion that the Incas—the great civilization that once occupied what is now Bolivia and Peru—extended much farther eastward than is generally imagined. The reasons I had for thinking that we need not go into now, but once when I was in England I read a lecture before a London society in which I stated these views, and to my disgust I was made to look a fool. The newspapers joined in the chorus of jeers, and that made me very angry, especially as none of my critics had even seen the country.

'Well, to make a long story short, I went back to the Matto Grosso—which is a province that occupies most of the vast hinterland of Brazil, stretching westwards to the Andes—determined to find proofs. I found them, too; in fact, I found more than I bargained for.' The old explorer leaned forward dramatically. 'I got on the trail of Atahuallpha's treasure,' he whispered mysteriously. 'The vast treasure of gold and precious stones that was being taken towards Cuzco by thousands of adoring priests for the ransom of Atahuallpha, their King, who was held prisoner by Pizarro, the Spaniard.

'You probably know the story of how Pizarro coolly murdered his captive, and how the priests, on hearing the news, turned about and hid the treasure so effectively that it has never been found, in spite of thousands of attempts that have been made to locate it. There is no doubt about the existence of the treasure, but I must admit it was certainly not in my mind when I discovered my first clue.'

'What was it?' muttered Biggles involuntarily.

Dickpa rose, crossed the room, opened a drawer in a desk, and returned with a rough oblong shaped piece of metal, which he flung on the table with a dull crash. 'Gold,' he said tersely, 'solid gold; and I picked it up at a place where the experts—save the word!—say no Incas ever came. I followed up the clue and found other things. Frankly, I was surprised, because I had always thought, as Mr. Prodgers, the great Andean explorer thought, the treasure was more likely to be farther north, in Ecuador.' Dickpa looked long and searchingly across the gardens, taking care not to expose himself, before he continued.

'Unfortunately, I had with me as carriers a very bad lot. Porters are difficult to obtain in Brazil at any time, and they are always unreliable. I had four men and an Indian-Brazilian, named Philippe Nunez, was the worst of the lot; a coward, a thief, and a liar. He is outside in the park somewhere at this moment.'

'Well, let's go and shoot him up,' suggested the practical Biggles instantly.

'Impossible,' declared Dickpa. 'It would be murder. How are we going to account to the police for dead bodies about the park?'

'Hm! I suppose you're right,' agreed Biggles reluctantly.

'These rascals,' continued Dickpa, 'got wind of what I had found and deserted me, taking all my food and stores with them—and there's little to be had there. I won't trouble you now with the harrowing details of my trip home, how I was found almost naked, and dying of starvation, by a rubber collector and taken down the river in his canoe, and then to Manaos, which, as you know, is a large town on the Amazon.

'Judge my amazement, when I got there, to find an expedition just leaving to recover the treasure, led, if

15

you please, by Philippe Nunez, my late porter, and an American wastrel named Silas Blattner. I was too ill with fever to do anything, but I was convalescent when the expedition returned. It had failed, and for the simple reason that, although Philippe knew roughly the locality of the treasure, he did not know the exact spot, and it was like looking for a needle in a haystack. At first I was mildly amused, but my amusement turned to alarm when they tried to kidnap me to force me to divulge my secret.

'I had ideas of forming another expedition, but I quickly discovered it was out of the question. Apart from the fact that the men I engaged were promptly bribed by the enemy to disclose my plans, it became clear that my life would not be worth a moment's purchase if I ventured far from civilization. Indeed, so desperate did matters become that I had no alternative but to flee the country. That's what it amounted to, and I'm not ashamed to admit it.

'I was puzzled for a long time to know how this gang—for it is nothing less—managed to get enough money to defray their expenses, but by employing their own methods—that is, by a little bribery—I discovered that they had behind them two of the wealthiest men in Brazil. These two men handle all the rubber from the upper Amazon, which is one of the biggest industries of the country, and for this reason they are known locally as the Rubber Kings. Quite apart from the treasure, they dislike me personally because they know that *I* know the methods they employ for rubber collecting, which is nothing more or less than slavery in its most brutal form.

'Anyway, I sent you a cable from Marseilles to say I was on my way home, and then came on here. Judge my astonishment when, within a week, I saw Blattner and Nunez in the park. I had a narrow escape, but I managed to get back to the house; I tried to ring up the police, only to find that the phone wires had been cut. The next move was when they tried to get into the house at night, but I nailed up the windows on the ground floor and got my guns out. I am a man of few wants, and the small staff I had, apparently thinking I was insane, soon left me. I let them go; it was not much use trying to explain the position to them. And that's how things stand at this moment. I am here alone with those villains in the park. You see, even if I could get out and ask for police protection, they would just fade away when the police appeared and return when they had gone. What can I do? I can't give them in charge, for I have no charge to offer against them.

'I tried to escape, leaving the house to take its chance, but each time I had to fight my way back, for these rogues do not hesitate to use their weapons. So there we are,' concluded the old man with a grim smile.

'Well, if anyone except you told me that tale I should say he was off his rocker,' declared Biggles emphatically, 'but, knowing you, I can only say I am glad we've rolled up to lend a hand. We shall even things up a bit, I hope. What do you think about it, Algy?'

'Same as you,' agreed Algy decisively. 'But what are we going to do about it?'

'It's difficult to see what can be done about it,' admitted Dickpa frankly. 'I don't feel like being run out of my own house, but at the same time I feel still less like living as a cat in a tree with a terrier at the bottom.'

Biggles nodded. 'I think you're right there,' he agreed. 'The obvious plan that occurs to me is to go out and let these toughs have a dose of their own medicine, but that, as you say, might only lead to

17

complications. The alternative seems to be to get away and lie low; they might clear off when they discovered you'd gone.'

'Yes, but they'll certainly follow me, and this state of affairs would only be repeated elsewhere. The ideal thing would be to give them the slip entirely and get back to South America while they are looking for me here.'

'South America?' echoed Biggles with a start.

'Of course. What else? I certainly do not propose to abandon my quest altogether on account of a band of cut-throats.'

'Going back into the enemy camp sounds a grim proposition to me,' muttered Biggles doubtfully.

'But I have friends there as well as enemies,' replied Dickpa.

'Well, you please yourself, but I should feel inclined to leave it alone if I were you,' advised Biggles. 'After all, you have plenty of money. Why risk a knife in the back to get more?'

Dickpa shrugged his shoulders. 'It isn't altogether the monetary value of the treasure that appeals to me; it is the historical value of what I know exists there.'

'I see,' replied Biggles slowly. 'Well, if you are determined to go back, the thing is to think of the quickest way of getting out there, getting the treasure, and then getting back.'

'Precisely!'

'Have you ever thought of flying?' enquired Biggles, after a moment's pause.

It was Dickpa's turn to start. 'I have not,' he said emphatically. 'Most certainly I have not. Do you for one moment suppose I am likely to risk my neck in one of your crazy contraptions?'

'You might do worse,' retorted Biggles, frowning. 'I

can't understand people like you. You take the most outrageous risks with crazy collectors, poisonous reptiles, wild beasts, fever, and goodness knows what else, yet you jib at the safest form of transport in the world.'

'But—'

'Never mind but,' broke in Biggles. 'It looks to me as if you haven't much choice if you don't want to be murdered *en route*. Dash it all, it seems to me the answer to the question.'

'Where would we fly to from here?' asked Dickpa doubtfully.

'To Liverpool, I expect, or to your point of embarkation, but, if it comes to that, I don't see why you shouldn't do the whole job by air—except, of course, the Atlantic crossing.*'

'Good heavens, man!'

'Well, why not?'

'What about the Atlantic, though?'

'Dash the Atlantic. I'm not flying over any oceans myself, so you needn't worry about that. We could fly to Liverpool, ship the plane to America, and go over ourselves by boat. We'd pick up our equipment again over the other side.'

'Why do you say "we"?'

'We three. Who else?'

'Then you'd come?'

'Of course we'd come. I was only saying to Algy as we came up the drive that I was about sick of loafing about. This proposition sounds interesting to me.'

'I don't know what to think about it,' muttered Dickpa anxiously. 'I think the best thing would be for.

---

* Regular Atlantic flights only became common during World War II. During the 1920's and 30's few aircraft had the range to cross with any safety.

you to work out a definite plan of action for the whole trip. Then we'll have a round table conference about it, and I'll decide if it sounds practicable. How's that?'

'Fine! But first of all you'd better tell me a few things about the Matey Grocer—'

'The *Matto Grosso*.'

'Sorry. Well, tell us about it, so that Algy and I can determine the best sort of aircraft to be employed.'

'Very well, let's take our coffee into the smoke-room. The atlas is there, and the windows command a better view of the grounds in case our besiegers try any funny stuff.'

'They won't find it so funny if they do,' growled Biggles, scowling, as they made their way to the long, low, oak-panelled hall which was used as a smoke-room.

Chapter 2
Dickpa Explains

'The Matto Grosso,' began Dickpa when they had made themselves comfortable, 'is nominally a province of Brazil. Actually it is almost the whole vast centre of the South American continent. To the north lies the Amazon, to the west the great Cordillera of the Andean Range, and to the south lies another vast tract of unexplored country. It is hard to describe in terms of figures the magnitude of the place. You see, Brazil is larger than the whole of the United States of America with most of Europe added to it. Try and grasp just what that means. The area of England is just over 50,000 square miles; Brazil covers 3¼ *million* square miles. The Matto Grosso is nearly a million square miles in extent, which means that it is nearly twenty times as large as England, and except for a few insignificant places it is unexplored. It is the wildest and least known country in the world today. Mighty unnamed mountains rise to high heaven, and rivers, so huge that the Thames would be no more than a ditch compared to them, thread their way across it. Its immensity is overpowering. It is a land of open plains and forests often larger than the United Kingdom, and inhabited by tribes, some of whom have not yet seen a white man. It is a land where distances are measured, not in miles or hundreds of miles, but *thousands* of miles and months of travel. It is a poor land and yet a rich land, poor in food-producing plants and animals but rich beyond calculation in minerals. Gold, silver, platinum, mercury, tin, lead, iron, copper, not to speak of diamonds, rubies, and other precious stones, are found, but, owing to the difficulties of obtaining labour and supplies, these are barely touched. The forests are full of valuable timbers, which remain there for the same reason. The greatest wealth of the country has come from the rubber, which, as you know, is collected from the trees which exist near the banks of the rivers, which are the only highways.'

'What are the weather conditions like?' asked Biggles with interest.

'On the uplands it can be cold at night, but, being in the tropics, the days are usually very hot. Storms of rain, such as we do not understand in this country, sweep across the country in the rainy season.'

'Any wild beasts—lions or things like that?' asked Algy anxiously.

Dickpa laughed. 'No lions,' he said. 'The jaguar is about the only animal of the cat family one need fear. There are many other wild animals, of course—queer beasts, most of them—but none to cause alarm. The rivers are full of crocodiles, and *pirhanas* are found in many places.'

'What are they?' asked Biggles with interest.

Dickpa looked grave for a moment. 'They are quite small fish about the size of herrings, but perhaps the most blood-thirsty little wretches in the world. They go about in huge shoals, and woe betide the unfortunate man who encounters them in the water. They are armed with sharp teeth, and have a grip like a bulldog that will take the piece right out of whatever they bite. They have been known to clean the flesh off a man's bones—or an animal's, if it comes to that—leaving only the white skeleton, in a matter of a few minutes. Even people wading have been attacked, and died from loss of blood before they could take the few steps necessary to reach the bank. The ferocity of their attack must be seen to be believed. One drop of blood in the water will fetch every *pirhana* for miles, and the natives fear them more than all the crocodiles and big water-snakes put together.'

'I can see I shan't do much swimming,' muttered Biggles with a grimace. 'And did you say snakes?'

'Oh, yes, you'll find snakes everywhere, both on the land and in the water, including some of the largest in the world. They often run upwards of twenty feet in length. I could tell you some queer tales about snakes,' mused the old explorer reflectively.

'I shouldn't, not unless you want me to change my mind about coming,' interposed Biggles.

'The snakes don't really matter; one soon gets accustomed to them,' went on Dickpa. 'The real pests are the insects, and they do scare me, I must confess. There are so many of them. There are bees which do not sting, but make your life a misery by crawling all over you—into your eyes, ears, nose, and even mouth.'

'We can fly higher than they can,' observed Biggles confidently.

'You might, but they'll be waiting for you when you land,' observed Dickpa drily. 'The ants are the very dickens. They are everywhere in countless myriads, in all colours and sizes. Sometimes they march about in columns, and sometimes they work independently, but they are always on the rampage. I don't know which are the worst, the big *saubas*, which are over an inch long and bite like the very devil, or the *cupim*, which are the notorious white ants and the most destructive creatures in the world. Nothing is safe from them. Leave your hat or coat on the ground at night and it will be gone in the morning, carried away in thousands

23

of tiny pieces. They eat the entire middles out of the trees, which is one of the reasons why trees are always crashing down in the forest. You must never forget the ant—not that they give you much chance of forgetting them—for they are the real rulers of the country.

'Then there are the *piums*, tiny beasts worse than mosquitoes which squirt a sort of acid into your eyes, and the *polvoras*—the name really means "powder," because they are so small. They fly about literally in billions and sting you all over. Worse still, perhaps, is the little horror known as the *carrapato*, which is a flat beast about the size of the end of a lead pencil. It has wonderful clinging powers by means of hooks on its feet. Its great object in life is to stick its head under your skin and suck your blood. The trouble is, you can't get it off. If you pull it the head breaks off and sticks in your skin and makes a nasty sore. The only way to get it out is with a pin.'

Dickpa paused to let his words sink in.

'Any more horrors?' asked Biggles.

'Plenty,' replied Dickpa, grinning. 'There are the *carrapatinhos*, which are the younger and perhaps more active brothers of the *carrapatos*.'

'Don't tell me about them,' broke in Biggles quickly.

'Sounds a good place for a picnic,' observed Algy drily. 'What is the country itself like—I mean as far as possible landing-places are concerned?'

'Well, that's a big question,' answered Dickpa. 'Like most other wild countries, you get a bit of everything; forest, swamp, and plain. Some of the country has to be seen to be believed. It is nearly all volcanic. Once upon a time, it must have been one colossal roaring furnace, with great craters throwing up ashes and lava for great distances. You'll find cinders everywhere, and great, round, queer-shaped stones which were once

24

molten rock, but have now solidified. In places the earth has sunk, leaving mighty masses of rock sticking up thousands of feet into the air. Goodness knows what is on top of them; in most places the walls rise up sheer from the plain, so it is impossible to climb them. There are places where formations like churches, castles, and other buildings can be seen. In my opinion, these are simply odd-shaped pinnacles of rock but one or two of the very few people who have been there think differently. Colonel Fawcett, for instance, spent years in the country, and was firmly convinced they were the ruins of a lost civilization. Poor fellow, he did not come back from his last journey. It is now almost certain that he and his son Jack were killed by hostile tribes in the interior. They disappeared, leaving no trace behind them. A well-equipped expedition has been out to look for them or to try and solve the mystery, but in vain.'

Dickpa paused to relight his pipe, which had gone out.

'Tell me this,' asked Biggles: 'what are our chances of landing near the treasure? I mean, is there a flat plain handy, or a large river or lake where a flying-boat or seaplane could be put down?'

'Both of them,' replied Dickpa quickly. 'The place is not far from a large river about a hundred yards wide, generally deep, but shallow in places. There are islands in it, and sandbanks at intervals. The actual ground in the district is flat enough, but there are boulders, ant-hills, and occasional patches of *matto*, or dwarf scrub, and forest.'

'The boulders and ant-hills sound awkward,' observed Biggles.

'I'm afraid they are scattered about almost everywhere,' nodded Dickpa, 'although there are, of course, plenty of places where you could land an aeroplane, if you knew where they were.'

'It doesn't sound very inviting, all the same,' mused Biggles. 'If we bumped into a boulder and bust the machine we should be in a bonny mess. But go on, Dickpa.'

'Well, generally speaking, that is what most of the country over which we should have to fly is like,' continued Dickpa. 'I do not profess to understand aviation, but I should think the rivers would be the safest places to land on, although you would have to be careful of waterfalls, rapids, and cataracts. In any case, in order to reach the place we should have to fly up the river, at least as far as Manaos, which is the best part of a thousand miles from the sea, in order to start as near as possible to our final destination with a full load of stores and petrol. I can wire to my agent there to get those things ready for us. You must understand there is nothing anywhere else, absolutely nothing except what I have told you. There are no habitations or places where food can be obtained. Isn't there some sort of aeroplane which can come down on both land and water? I seem to remember seeing pictures of such a machine in the papers, a—a—what was it called?'

'Amphibian,' said Biggles quickly.

'That's right,' said Dickpa. 'But perhaps I had better tell you that the actual treasure is on, or rather in, a hill. I'll tell you how I stumbled on it, then you'll get a better grasp of the whole thing.' Dickpa filled his pipe and settled a little deeper in his chair before he continued.

'I was exploring a tributary of the Madeira River, which in turn is a tributary of the Amazon, travelling, of course, by canoe. The difficulties of travelling overland are almost insurmountable. I had four porters with me, as I have told you, and a pretty lot of cutthroats they were. I had already overhead them discussing the possibility of murdering me and stealing my kit, and you can readily imagine that travelling in these circumstances becomes a bit of a strain. We were in an interesting stretch of country. If you look at the maps of the district—such as they are—you will see mountain ranges dotted about. They are usually shown in the maps many miles from where they really are; indeed, I came to the conclusion years ago that most of the physical features shown on the maps are just stuck in by the map-makers for decoration.

'I had wandered away along such a range of mountains and came to the side of a steep cliff, which rose perhaps a thousand feet or so above the small stream along which I was walking. As far as I know, no living people had ever been there before, the nearest being the Bororo Indians, who at that time had a settlement about a hundred miles to the north. These Indian tribes are nomadic; that is, they wander about the country choosing new sites for their camp from time to time. They burn the undergrowth, dig the earth, plant their *mingao*, or corn, and then, as the jungle closes in on it, which it soon does, they move along to a fresh place. The only clothes they wear are big macaw and parrot feathers stuck in their hair. They are an unwelcoming lot, and I was quite glad they were some way away and that I was in a district where, as far as I knew, they never came.

'I was just passing a big fissure, or crack in the rock, when my eye fell on something that pulled me up with a jerk. It was a rock carving, quite small and simple— the sort of device a schoolboy might make with a penknife while he was idly waiting for somebody. I took a closer look and nearly let out a yell, for the design, which represented the rising sun, was characteristically of Inca origin. It was definite proof of my theories, as it showed conclusively that an Inca army, or a soldier at least, had penetrated as far westward. I hunted around looking for more, but in vain, and then I thought that something might be found in the cleft itself, so in I went. The first thing I stumbled on was a piece of pottery, also unmistakably of Inca manufacture. Striking matches, I advanced, and soon picked up a copper spear. That settled it, for the Incas were the only people to discover the secret of tempering copper to steel-like hardness.

'As you can imagine, I began to see I was on the track of something. The cleft had by this time widened out into quite a cave, and I went on slowly. Then I saw a small oblong-shaped article lying at my feet. I picked it up, and when I felt its weight I didn't have to look to see what it was.' Dickpa leaned forward dramatically.

'Gold,' he whispered, 'a lump of solid gold. It was, in fact, the piece I have already shown you. Then I got a facer. The cave came to an abrupt end. From side to side and from floor to ceiling was a wall that had obviously been built by the hand of man. It was formed of great blocks of stone morticed together without mortar, and fitting so tightly that you couldn't get a knife-blade between them. Only one race in the world could do that. Incas! Bolivia and Peru abound in walls and buildings constructed in the same way.

'Well, there it was. What lay behind the wall? I didn't know, but I could guess. Obviously they hadn't built a wall like that just there for fun. No, it hid something the builders were anxious to hide, and the bar of gold I had found told its own story. They had left a guard at the entrance while they were working, and he, in a fit of absent-mindedness, had carelessly left a mark that betrayed the secret.

'Trembling with excitement, I hurried back to the entrance of the cave, and reached it just as my last match went out. I had been in there longer than I thought, and it was nearly dark outside. However, I reached camp and found things in a serious state; my men were having one of their regular mutinies, but one glance showed me it was worse than usual. Philippe came up to me with a nasty scowl on his face and told me he wouldn't go on any farther; the men wanted their pay and were going home. I gave them their money and told them they could get off as soon as they liked and I hoped they'd enjoy being killed by Indians. That was the usual way I met their demands, and from experience I knew perfectly well that when it came to the pinch they wouldn't go, because without me they knew they'd stand a jolly poor chance of getting through.

'Then a tragedy happened. I was taking off my coat, to wash, when the material, rotten with the damp heat, broke under the weight of the gold which was in the pocket and the lump of yellow metal fell to the ground. Philippe broke off in the middle of a sentence and stared at it, fascinated. Then he dragged his eyes away and looked at me. He knew what it was, for I saw a look of greed and hatred in his eyes. I picked it up carelessly, as if it was nothing important, but it didn't deceive him, and presently I saw him in earnest conversation with the others. I was in a pretty pickle, and I knew it. It was out of the question to think of breaking down the wall in the cave, for my men would never now let me out of their sight, and if once they saw what I suspected was behind that wall, my life wouldn't be worth a moment's purchase. Luckily they did not know where the place was. What to do I didn't know, but finally I slung my hammock as usual some distance from the men and went to bed to think it over.

'I slept with one eye open, as the saying goes—I had become pretty adept at it. I wasn't in the least surprised when, just after midnight, I saw a dark shadow crawling towards me in the moonlight. As it came nearer I saw it was Philippe, his face distorted horribly by a knife he held in his teeth. Pretending to be sound asleep, I felt quietly for my revolver and let him come on. I waited until he was about ten yards away, and then, with a shout, I sprang from the hammock. He jumped to his feet and would have bolted like the coward he was, but I was furious and fetched him an upper cut to the point of the jaw. He took a frightful purler, and the knife flew out of his mouth, but he picked himself up and ran off moaning. I let him go—what else could I do? I couldn't make a prisoner of him in such a place, and to shoot the man would have meant serious trouble with the Brazilian authorities.

'I heard a babble of voices as he reached the others and then the clicking of rifles being loaded—they had insisted upon being armed as a protection against the Indians. I called out to them that I would shoot the first man who showed himself before daylight, and, knowing I should be as good as my word, they drew off, muttering. As you can well imagine, I didn't have much sleep for the rest of the night, but towards morning I must have dozed off, for when next I opened my eyes it was just getting daylight. I thought everything sounded very quiet; there was none of the usual grumbling and cursing of the men loading the canoe. I was soon to discover the reason. They had gone. And that was not all. Gone, too, were all my stores, everything except the clothes I stood up in. I was alone in the forest, more than five hundred miles from the nearest point of civilization. I don't mind admitting I was pretty well stunned for a bit, as I had no delusions about what that meant. I thought I was a goner, and that's a fact. Death from starvation or in a dozen other ways stared me in the face. If you have ideas about reaching out and picking bananas or coconuts in Brazil, forget it. What few edible fruits and nuts there are exist only on the tops of the trees, where the birds and monkeys alone can reach them. Those that fall to the ground are immediately carried away piecemeal by the ants.

'By a marvellous bit of luck I had in my pocket a fishing-line and hook which I had taken with me the day before in case I saw fish in the stream. I cut a bamboo for a rod, and, using a small piece of biscuit—also fortunately left over from the day before—for bait, I soon had a ten-pounder of the sort locally known as a *pintado* on the bank.

'You'll believe me when I tell you that my adventures on the rest of that trip, which took nearly six months, would fill a book. What with fever and hunger—I often went days on end with nothing past my lips—I was not exactly a pretty specimen when I was discovered by a rubber collector and taken to his hut. As soon as I was able to get on my feet I made my way slowly down the river to Manaos. There, as I told you, I got another shock when I discovered my late carriers and two Americans, Blattner and a fellow named Steinburg, setting off to find the treasure. They failed, and the rest you know. The point is, what is the next move?' concluded Dickpa, leaning back and once more reaching for his tobacco-pouch.

Biggles pondered deeply for a few minutes. 'Frankly, I see no reason why this trip to the Mater Grasso—'

'*Matto Grosso*,' corrected Dickpa again.

'Sorry. Well, I don't see why it shouldn't be undertaken by aeroplane, but it will cost a lot of money.'

'It would cost that anyway,' declared Dickpa. 'On my last trip I spent thousands of pounds on equipment. Why, I had to pay my porters a pound* a day, and feed them, and food up there costs its weight in gold.'

'All right, then,' said Biggles conclusively, 'If you're willing to foot the bill I'll tell you what we'll do. I'll get away from here after dark, leaving Algy to help you hold the fort, so to speak. You give me an open cheque on your bank and some money for expenses, and I'll buy a four-seater amphibian and the rest of the equipment we are likely to require. I'll look up Smyth—he was my mechanic in France—and get him to come with us. I don't think he'll need much persuading. I'll have the machine shipped to New York on a mail packet, and Smyth can go with it. Then I'll come back here in a hired machine, arriving about dawn, and pick you up in that long meadow at the end of the garden. I ought to be able to get back here in a week. We'll fix the date later.

'The night before I'm due to arrive, you and Algy pack up here, creep out under cover of darkness, and lie doggo on the edge of the field. As soon as my wheels touch, you break cover and sprint towards me. With any luck you ought to be aboard and away before Silas and his toughs spot the game. The big advantage of using an aeroplane for this is that they won't know which way we've gone. Once in the air we shall make straight for Liverpool, hand over the machine, and get aboard a boat bound for America. As soon as we get there we'll assemble the machine and push off down the east coast of South America on the way to Manaos.

* Worth perhaps seventy-five pounds today.

You, Dickpa, can cable your agent from Liverpool to lay in a stock of juice* and tinned grub. How's that?'

'Sounds good to me,' agreed Algy.

'Well, you boys know more about it than I do, and I am willing to place myself in your hands,' said Dickpa. 'There are certain formalities to be arranged; you can't just go crashing about in other people's countries without a permit.'

'We shall leave that to you,' said Biggles promptly. 'You know the ropes, and can handle that while we're fixing up about the machine.'

'Splendid,' agreed Dickpa, his eyes shining. 'It would give me the greatest pleasure to outwit these villains after all. When do you propose to start?'

'Tonight. We've decided to go on with this, so there is no point in wasting time. The sooner we get a move on the better; besides, you'll soon be running short of food, I expect.'

'That suits me,' agreed Algy. 'I can send a wire to my people from Liverpool telling them I have gone off on a holiday and they can expect me back when they see me.'

'That's about the wisest thing you *could* tell them,' said Dickpa grimly. 'I hope neither of you have the idea that this is going to be altogether a picnic. Knowing what I know about South America, I should say there are exciting times ahead.'

Even so, he little guessed just how exciting they were to be.

* Slang: petrol.

Chapter 3
Running The Gauntlet

The grandfather clock in the hall had just struck ten when Biggles pushed his chair back, rose to his feet, and buttoned up his coat. 'Well,' he said, 'I'll be off before the moon gets up; this is the darkest it will be tonight.'

Dickpa looked at him anxiously, half inclined to withdraw from the venture which would put his nephew's life in jeopardy at the very onset. 'For goodness' sakes be careful,' he cautioned him, 'and don't make the mistake of under-estimating these fellows outside. They're used to using their guns in their own country, and will stop at nothing to get what they want.'

Biggles frowned. 'If they try any rough stuff on me, they'll get as good as they give,' he said shortly. 'You'll probably have a tougher proposition to face here,' he added, putting on his hat and turning his coat over his white collar. 'Algy can augment your supplies by sneaking out at night and getting fruit and vegetables out of the garden.'

'Yes, we might do that,' admitted Dickpa. 'How are you thinking of getting out of the house?'

'Through the kitchen window,' replied Biggles. 'I've had a good look round, and that seems to me to be the best place. There is only one small section of the paddock that overlooks it, and it lets me straight out into a thick clump of lilac-bushes.'

'What about weapons?' asked Dickpa.

Biggles shook his head dubiously. 'Better without 'em—at least, without firearms,' he replied. 'What's the use? Even if there is a rough house, I can't very well use a gun; the police court proceedings would put the tin hat on the whole affair right away. If I happened to kill a Brazilian, it would hardly do to go to Brazil afterwards; I expect they'd make it pretty warm for me.'

'You're right there,' agreed Dickpa, 'and I think you're wise. Well, good-bye, old boy; take care of yourself. We shall be waiting for you today week at dawn, on the edge of the spinney by the long meadow.'

'That's it,' agreed Biggles, forcing the nailed-up kitchen window open as quietly as possible, using the tongs from the fireplace as a lever.

He peered long and steadily into the darkness. 'It seems quiet enough,' he whispered, throwing one leg over the window-sill. 'Cheerio, Dickpa. Cheerio, Algy,' he breathed, and a moment later he was swallowed up in the darkness of the night.

At the edge of the bushes he stood still and listened intently before crossing the exposed drive to the shrubbery beyond. He glanced upwards. A few stars were shining dimly, and, although the moon had not yet risen, there was just enough light to see without fear of colliding with obstacles. Slowly and with infinite care he parted the bushes and peered out. There was not a soul in sight; the only sound was the dismal hooting of an owl in the nearby spinney.

Swiftly but quietly he darted across the drive, freezing into immobility when he reached the deep gloom of the shrubbery on the other side. Was it or was it not? Had he seen a movement in the bushes a little lower down? He was not sure, for he knew only too well how easily one's imagination can play tricks at night when the nerves are stretched taut.

Suddenly, not far away, a twig cracked, and he knew he had not been mistaken. In spite of his coolness his heart beat a trifle faster and a curious gleam came into his eyes, the look they had worn when, not so long before, they had peered through the Alvis sight of the twin Vickers guns on the cowling of his Sopwith Camel.*

'It begins to look as if Dickpa's right,' he thought, for the enemy evidently kept good watch. With his left hand advanced to prevent collision with an unseen obstacle, he stealthily edged his way a few paces farther on. Another twig cracked, closer this time. Again Biggles stood stock still, eyes straining into the darkness, trying to make out the direction from which the sound had come. He thought it came from the right, but a moment later a bush rustled softly on his left and he caught his breath sharply. It began to look as if his exit had been seen after all and the enemy were closing in on him.

His lips set in the thin, straight line peculiar to him in moments of impending action. Intuition warned him that something was going to happen, and he was not mistaken. The blinding beam of a flash-lamp stabbed the darkness, swept round swiftly in a short arc, and came to rest on him. Instantly he dropped to his knees. He was not a moment too soon. Something heavy whistled through the air over his head. He leapt sideways like a cat and collided head-on with a figure that loomed up before him. Acting with the speed of light, he brought his fist up with a vicious jab into the pit of

* A World War I single-seater biplane fighter armed with twin Vickers machine guns synchronized to fire through the propeller.

36

the man's stomach. There was a choking grunt as the man collapsed, clutching feebly at Biggles's legs as he fell, but the pilot, thinking and acting simultaneously at the speed that air combat had taught him, was no longer there.

Casting all pretence at concealment to the winds, he darted away through the bushes, dodging and twisting like a snipe. He heard the heavy crash of a revolver; out of the corner of his eye he saw the blaze of the flash and heard the bullet rip through the branches just above his head. 'Like old times,' he found time to mutter to himself as he broke through the far side of the bushes and sprinted along the edge. For a few minutes he heard sounds of pursuit; shouts, curses, and the crash of bodies plunging through bushes. Again the revolver barked, and his lips parted in a smile as he heard an angry shout in answer, warning the gunman to be careful where he was shooting. 'Algy looks like having a warm time if he tries any raspberry picking,' he thought as, with his eyes fixed ahead, he ran on.

Presently the sounds of pursuit died down behind him and he slowed down to take his bearings. He decided that he must have broken through the cordon, and with great satisfaction headed towards the nearest village at a steady trot.

Meanwhile Dickpa and Algy had stood staring at the open window through which Biggles had disappeared, the former with obvious anxiety and the latter with supreme confidence born of long experience in far greater perils.

'I hope I have done the right thing,' breathed Dickpa. 'I should never forgive myself if, after all he has been through—'

'I shouldn't worry,' broke in Algy. 'Biggles can take care of himself, never fear.'

For some time they stood in silence, listening for any sound that might indicate the discovery of the adventurer, but all was still.

'I think he must have got through,' whispered Dickpa with a sigh of relief.

He had hardly spoken the words when there came a sudden shout, and a revolver blazed in the darkness outside.

Dickpa seized Algy's arm in a vice-like grip. 'That's done it,' he groaned.

'Certainly not,' replied Algy shortly. 'Biggles has been shot at before, don't forget.'

Again they stood listening, trying to hear some sound which might let them know whether Biggles had been captured or whether he had escaped.

'Shh!' breathed Algy. 'Don't move. Under the apple-tree, over in the corner—I saw a movement. Look! There's another of them—over by the yew hedge. They're making for the house. All right, we'll give them something to think about.' He hurried through to the hall, closely followed by Dickpa, and picked up the heavy elephant gun. 'Is it loaded?' he asked quickly.

'Yes,' replied Dickpa, 'but—'

'That's all right,' muttered Algy. 'I'm not going to kill anybody.' And, turning, ran quickly up the stair-case. He entered the door of a bedroom that commanded a view from the front of the house and opened the window quietly. Not a sound broke the stillness of the summer night.

'There's one of them,' breathed Dickpa suddenly, 'over there under the rhododendron-bushes.'

'I see him; leave him to me,' whispered Algy. He

took quick aim at the tops of the bushes and pulled the trigger.

The roar of the great gun shattered the silence in a mighty volume of sound that seemed to shake even the house to its foundations. A full minute elapsed before the echoes had died away.

'Listen out there!' called Algy crisply. 'I'm giving you fair warning that the first man who puts foot within twenty yards of this house will get a dose of hot lead.'

Into the silence that followed, a sound of crashing and stumbling came from several places among the bushes.

Algy smiled. 'That should give them something to think about, anyway,' he muttered grimly. 'All the same,' he went on, 'I shall be glad when the week is up; it's going to be pretty monotonous sitting here doing nothing except keep guard.'

Chapter 4

The Getaway

The stars were paling in the faint grey light that crept upward in the eastern sky and heralded the coming of dawn. Somewhere in the thick coppice that bordered the long pasture a bird chirped suddenly, then another, and another. A blackbird burst out of the hedge with a shrill clamour of alarm.

'Dash that bird,' muttered Algy irritably from where he crouched low in a thicket near the edge of the wood. 'It will give the game away if we aren't careful.'

Dickpa looked up from where he was sitting huddled on a suitcase, and nodded. 'I hope to goodness he comes,' he whispered. 'I'm wondering how we shall get back to the house if he doesn't.'

'I shouldn't waste time thinking about that,' whispered Algy; 'you evidently don't know Biggles. He'll come all right. Thank goodness there's no ground mist. That's the only thing that worried me. Just pray for the weather conditions to keep fine; that's the most important thing.'

A week had passed since Biggles had departed on his quest, and, in accordance with their plans, Dickpa and Algy had made their way to the rendezvous, to await Biggles's arrival in the promised aircraft. Fortunately the night had been dark, and, leaving the house by a side window soon after midnight, they had been able to worm their way to the appointed place. It had been nerve-racking work, for in the interval of time they had seen members of the enemy camp repeatedly, and it was obvious that the siege was being maintained.

The early morning air was chilly, and Algy watched the sky anxiously. Slowly the light grew stronger, and a bright patch of turquoise appeared overhead as the sun rose over the horizon.

'Hark!' Algy turned his head in a listening position and his heart gave a throb of excitement as faintly, from the far distance, the unmistakable sound of an aero engine reached their ears.

'He's coming!' Dickpa's voice literally trembled with excitement.

For answer, Algy pointed to a tiny speck in the sky which his practised eye had picked out. It was approaching rapidly, and any doubts that they might have had that it was not Biggles, but another wandering airman, were soon set at rest, for it was heading straight towards them.

'Don't move until his wheels touch,' warned Algy. The noise of the engine died away abruptly and the machine began to side-slip* steeply towards the field in which they crouched. 'I expect other eyes besides ours are watching him,' went on Algy. 'We shall have to sprint for all we are worth when we do move.'

The machine, under expert handling, swung round up the field, levelled out, and dropped as lightly as a feather upon the dewy turf about a hundred yards away in a perfect three-point landing.**

'Come on, Dickpa, run for it,' muttered Algy, picking up a bulky bundle from the ground at their feet, which contained the few articles that Dickpa considered

* A sideways movement of the aircraft, used, in this case, to lose height quickly.
** A landing where the two forward landing wheels and the tailwheel (also called the tail skid) all touch the ground together.

indispensable. 'Never mind me; run straight to the machine.'

Side by side they broke from the bushes and ran towards the machine, still ticking over where it had landed. The pilot saw them almost at once, opened his engine with a roar, and taxied quickly towards them.

The runners heard him yell something, but what he said was drowned in the noise of the engine and the whip-like crack of the revolver from somewhere behind them. Without pausing in his stride, Algy snatched a fleeting glance over his shoulder; three men were just emerging from the edge of the wood, one of them firing a revolver as he ran.

Panting, Algy reached the machine. 'In you go, Dickpa,' he snapped, and swung lightly into the seat, dragging Dickpa in head first behind him. He ducked as a bullet zipped through the canvas fuselage just behind him.

But the machine was already moving forward under the swelling roar of the engine; the tail rose as it raced across the turf like an arrow. Bump—bump—bump— it rocked over grass-covered mole-hills, and Algy stared aghast at the line of trees ahead. Would she never lift? He saw at a glance that it was going to be a close thing.

Biggles, sitting tense in his cockpit, had his eyes riveted on the formidable line of trees and knew it was going to be touch and go whether they cleared them or not. He held the stick forward until the last moment to get as much speed as possible, and then, when collision seemed inevitable, jerked it back into his stomach. He held his breath while the under-carriage wheels literally grazed the topmost branches and the machine hung for a moment as if undecided whether to stall or go on.

Algy felt the aeroplane wobble as the controls

relaxed, and then sank back limply as it picked up again, knowing only too well how near they had been to disaster at the very onset of their quest. He pulled on the helmet and goggles the pilot had thoughtfully placed in the cockpit in readiness, and a moment later saw Dickpa's head similarly garbed. Biggles looked back over his shoulder and grinned at his passengers. Then he held his left hand high in the air, thumb turned upwards, with a triumphant gesture, and they returned the thumbs-up salute, which means the same thing the whole world over.

Chapter 5
Trouble

With his altimeter registering five thousand feet, Biggles looked a trifle apprehensively over the side of his cockpit at the unusual scene below as he headed westwards in a Vickers Amphibian. Immediately below, a broad, winding silver ribbon marked the course of the mighty Amazon, the largest river in the world. On both sides lay the forest, dark and unfathomable, like a great sombre pall over the face of the earth, merging into vague purple and blue shadows at the remote horizon. There was nothing else; not a road, a field, or an isolated tree that might be taken for a landmark. The utter sameness of it all had appalled him at first, but now he was growing accustomed to it, for they were far up the river, approaching Manaos, the strange city founded by gold-hunting pioneers hundreds of years ago in the savage heart of a savage continent.

Biggles glanced at Algy, sitting in the second pilot's seat at his left hand, and smiled, for their plans had gone like clockwork since they had left England a month before. Even the weather had been on its best behaviour. They had taken ship at Liverpool, and on arrival at New York found the huge case containing the amphibian that Biggles had purchased had already been opened by the industrious Smyth, Biggles's old flight-sergeant mechanic of 266 Squadron,* and the machine awaiting erection.

* See Biggles of the Fighter Squadron, published by Red Fox.

Algy had glanced over her lines while Biggles explained the reason for his choice. She was a five-seater that had been specially built for a wealthy private owner who had been killed in an accident on a motor race track before he had even time to take delivery. Consequently Biggles had been able to get a bargain. The open side-by-side cockpits in the nose, with dual controls, could be reached from the snug enclosed cabin in the boat-shaped hull. The cabin itself was luxuriously equipped for three passengers, but Biggles had had most of the unnecessary furniture removed to lighten the load and make room for the spare parts, equipment, and stores necessary for their adventure. A rather elaborate case containing four parachutes he had left untouched, as well as a cabinet holding a Very pistol,* signal flares, and navigation instruments. The machine was a biplane, with the engine mounted between the wings, and of the 'pusher' type—that is, with the propeller behind the engine.

The single Bristol Jupiter engine gave a maximum speed of a hundred and twenty miles an hour and a cruising speed of a hundred and five—ample for their requirements, since speed was not a matter of such importance as reliability. The aircraft had been originally designed for an endurance range of nearly a thousand miles, but Biggles, bearing in mind the nature of the country they were visiting, had had an extra tank fitted which would give them a further five hundred miles if desired. The undercarriage was of the retractable type—that is to say, it could be lowered or raised at the will of the pilot according to whether he wished to come down on land or water.

---

* A short-barrelled pistol for firing coloured flares for signalling and sending messages. Especially useful before the days of radio in planes.

Algy agreed that Biggles had just cause to be proud of his bargain, for it could not have suited their purpose better had it been specially designed for the undertaking. There had been some discussion about the selection of a suitable name, but the choice had finally been left to Dickpa, who had decided on the *Condor*, after the huge bird of that name which makes its home in the mighty Andean Range.

A fortnight's hard work and the machine was ready to take the air. The tests were satisfactory in every way, and they had forthwith taken off on the long voyage southwards to the land of their quest.

Biggles nudged his flying partner and nodded, his eyes fixed on a spot directly ahead, and Algy, following his glance, saw in the distance an expanse of white buildings which he knew must be Manaos, their immediate destination and the last point of civilization they would touch before plunging into the wilds of the vast Brazilian hinterland.

The landing of the amphibian caused a considerable commotion, people hurrying from their homes to the waterside, and it was clear that an aeroplane was a very rare bird in the town so far removed from civilization. Canoes and other small craft flocked about them as the pilot taxied slowly towards what seemed to be a suitable anchorage, and, in spite of the warning shouts of Dickpa, who had climbed out on to the hull, some of them were in imminent danger of being run down.

A small launch spluttered up, with an official in a gaudy uniform standing in the bows. He shouted something unintelligible to Biggles, but Dickpa evidently understood, for he cautioned the pilot to stop.

'I'm afraid he's going to be awkward,' he said, frowning. 'That's the worst of these fellows,' he added; 'they

46

must exercise their powers on every possible occasion. We shall have to listen to what he has to say.'

The appearance of the official did not improve at close quarters. His uniform had been hastily flung on over a suit of pyjamas that were none too clean, while his face, which was unshaven, was flushed with anger.

'What do you mean, landing at this hour?' he stormed. 'Don't you know I always rest at this time? You would not dare to treat the officers in your own country in this way—' He broke off with a start and stared at Dickpa with a flash of recognition in his eyes. 'Ah!' he said softly, and then again, 'Ah! It's you, is it?' He scowled malevolently, and, before Dickpa could frame a suitable answer, he had snapped an order to the man at the wheel. The launch swung round, nearly fouling the fragile side of the amphibian as it did so, and headed back towards the shore at full speed.

Dickpa, a frown puckering his brow, watched the departing official in perplexity. 'He's new to me,' he muttered, 'but he seems to know me and I strongly suspect he's going to make things as awkward for us as he can. Never mind; it can't be helped. Taxi to the bank and let me get ashore. The sooner I find my agent and ask him if he got my cable about a supply of petrol the better. If he did, we had better see about refuelling at once. I'm rather afraid we've made a mistake in coming here at all, but it was difficult to see how we could manage for oil and petrol by doing otherwise. If the men who are financing the enemy are in the town, they'll know I am here, and why. Yes, you'll have to put me ashore; the rest of you must stay aboard and look after the machine until I come back. I shall soon find out how the land lies.'

Still followed by a crowd of natives in small boats, they taxied in and dropped anchor near the bank.

47

Dickpa beckoned one of the boats nearer, jumped aboard, and, after rattling some brief instruction to the startled native, was quickly put ashore. With a parting wave he disappeared in the direction of a row of small shops near the water-front.

'I don't like the look of this,' muttered Biggles to Algy as they watched Dickpa's disappearing figure. 'Some of these people look capable of anything. Well, we might as well make ourselves as comfortable as we can until he comes back. My word, it's pretty hot down here on the floor, isn't it?'

An hour passed slowly, and another, but still there was no sign of Dickpa, and Biggles's face began to wear a worried look. 'I don't like this,' he said again; 'I've a feeling in my bones that there's mischief brewing. If there is, and they try any funny stuff, they'll be sorry, that's all. That petrol would have been here an hour ago if everything had been all right,' he concluded.

Algy nodded assent from where he sat watching Smyth making a minor adjustment to a turnbuckle.* 'It'll be dark in half an hour, too,' he went on, with a quick glance at the sky. 'Hello, what's this coming?'

A small launch had put off from the shore and was chugging its way quickly and with scant ceremony through the still lingering spectators in their miscellaneous assortment of small craft. It pulled up alongside, and they saw at once that there was only one man in it, an elderly white man in well-worn ducks** and a battered solar topee.

'Which of you is Bigglesworth?' he asked sharply.

---

* A fitting used to adjust the tension of wires to which it is attached. Used a lot for wing and internal bracing wires in biplanes.
** Word used to describe a lightweight linen suit often worn in very hot climates.

'I'm Carter, your uncle's agent. Speak up. You've no time to lose.'

Biggles stepped forward quickly and helped their visitor on board. 'I'm your man,' he said quickly. 'What's wrong?'

'Everything—no, don't talk; listen,' he went on with a hurried glance towards the shore. 'Major Bigglesworth, I'm sorry to say that your uncle is in jail.'

'In jail!' echoed Biggles incredulously. 'But—'

'It looks to me as if you're up against it properly,' broke in Carter, mopping his perspiring, fever-drawn face with a large yellow handkerchief. 'Luckily I was able to have a word with your uncle before they took him away. When I got his cable about the petrol I kept my mouth shut, because, being on the spot, I knew what was going on out here, and had a pretty shrewd idea of what this gang of crooks who are up against him were planning. By a stroke of luck I got hold of the petrol before they put an embargo on it, but they don't know that.'

'Who's "they"?' asked Biggles quickly.

'Joseph da Silva, the Mayor, and the best-hated man in Manaos. He's a tyrant in every sense of the word, and, like many of these local officials, can easily be bought. The crooks have oiled his palm to some purpose, and he's out to stop you. He's clapped your uncle in jail on the ridiculous pretext that his papers are not in order. It's utter bosh, of course, and the British Consul in Rio de Janeiro will soon put matters right when it reaches his ears, but that will all take time, which is just what da Silva is playing for, until the rest of the gang get back from Europe.

'Meanwhile, da Silva is cock of the walk here, don't make any mistake about that. What he says goes, without any argument, because he's got a mob of hooligans

49

dressed up in uniform which he calls police, but it is really a private bodyguard paid for out of trumped-up taxes and fines on Europeans like you and myself. Now about this petrol. It would be fatal for me to try and get it to you here. They'd stop me and collar the lot. Your only chance is to get off down the river, and I'll bring it to you there. You might be able to drift down after dark without being spotted, which would be so much the better, but I doubt if they'll leave you here as long as that. Da Silva would be quite good enough to throw the lot of you into prison and then smash your machine before you could get out. He knows he's safe. All you could do would be to complain to the Government afterwards, and if you knew as much about them as I do you wouldn't waste your time even doing that. You'll get no change out of anybody here. Now listen. About two miles below the town you'll see a creek on the same side, with a ruined overgrown hut on the bank. You get off down there and wait until I come. The petrol is in two-gallon tins. I'll load it up in my old Ford and bring it down by a track that leads to the place. Once you've got it, get it into your tanks as fast as you can. I shall have to slip back into the town, because they know I'm your uncle's agent and will probably be watching me. They may be watching me now, and if they find I'm playing into your hands I shall probably land in jail myself, or get a knife between my shoulder-blades.'

'Bad as that, are they?' muttered Biggles grimly.

'Worse!'

'What about Dickpa—I mean my uncle—though?'

'That's a bigger problem. You've got to get him out of that jail, and quickly, though how it's going to be done is more than I can say.'

'Where is this jail or whatever it is?'

50

'In the middle of the town; at the corner of the Cathedral and the Stretta Fontana. You can't mistake the street, because there's a double row of palms on either side. I dropped one of the policemen a couple of dollars and he told me they're keeping him there until tomorrow, as da Silva wants to talk to him. Then, unless he tells the Mayor something he·wants to know, they are going to take him to the proper jail in the native end of the town. If they ever get him in there, you'll never see him again. It's full of criminals, the scum of the earth, and half of them rotting with fever, leprosy, and God knows what other horrors. It's a pest-house, not a jail. If you want to see him alive again you'll have to get him out tonight.'

'In that case he's coming out tonight,' muttered Biggles through set teeth, 'and God help Mr. Slimy da Silva if he gets in my way. Thanks very much, Mr. Carter. It's jolly good of you to take all these risks for us. We shan't forget it.'

'Well, you get off down the river as fast as you can before they come after you. They'd tear this machine to bits if they got their hands on it, to prevent you going on with this business. And, by the way, I found out from the post office that Blattner and Steinburg are in New Orleans. Apparently they guessed as soon as you gave them the slip in England that you'd make for here, and they started off back as hard as they could come. Why they went by New Orleans is more than I can say, but they'll be here shortly, you can bet your boots on that.'

'I see,' replied Biggles. 'Well, you get off back now before you get into trouble. Dickpa left your address with us in case things went wrong, but I shan't worry you unless it is unavoidable. If things become serious, I should be glad if you would get a message down to

51

the Consul at Rio. I should hate to see you get pulled into the jail, too, through trying to help us.'

'Rot! Never mind about that; we're bound to stick to each other. If one Englishman can't help another in a case like this, it's a poor show.'

'That's the way to talk,' agreed Biggles. 'What time will you be along with the petrol?'

'As soon after dark as I can manage it.'

'Fine. We'll be there. Goodbye. See you later.'

Biggles watched the launch until it reached the bank before he turned to the others with a queer grimace. 'It looks as if we've got to get busy—'

'By Jingo it does!' cried Algy, starting up and pointing towards the bank some distance above the place where Carter had just gone ashore. 'He was only just in time. I don't like the look of this little lot coming now.'

Biggles swung round on his heel and took one look at a large launch that was churning the river into foam as it sped towards them. A group of men in uniform stood near the bow. 'Swing the prop, Smyth,' he snapped, dropping into his seat and grabbing the self-starter.

The mechanic swung the heavy metal propeller to fill the cylinders of the engine with gas, and then leapt away to the aft cockpit. 'Contact!' he cried.

'Gr-r-r-r-r-r-r-r,' whirred the self-starter, and with a bellow of sound the engine sprang to life. A shout from the rapidly approaching launch reached Biggles's ears, but he ignored it. The amphibian moved forward, slowly at first, but with ever-increasing speed. Turning in a wide curve as it reached the middle of the river, it sped like an arrow down the stream, leaving a broad ribbon of creamy foam in its wake.

A shot rang out, and the vicious rip of a bullet

through the top plane brought a snarl to Biggles's lips. 'You murdering hounds!' he choked, and pushed the throttle wide open. The amphibian leapt forward like a live thing, skimmed along the surface of the water for a moment, and then rose gracefully into the air, climbing steeply. Two minutes later, still climbing, Biggles saw the creek, with the ruined hut on its bank, below him; he did not stop, but flew on into the quickly fading light. Not until he was several miles below the town did he turn, throttle back, and start a long glide back towards the rendezvous.

Darkness fell with tropical suddenness just as the keel of the *Condor* broke the surface of the river just below the deserted creek. The pilot listened intently for a moment, and then, as there seemed to be no sign of pursuit, he taxied into the creek itself and switched off.

'Well, that's that,' he muttered, relieved, for the prospect of landing after dark on a strange, crocodile-infested river did not fill him with enthusiasm. He had not touched his engine since he began the glide down, so he hoped that their landing had passed both unseen and unheard. Fortunately the machine had finished its run quite close to the bank, so there was no need to taxi, the gentle current carrying them down until they rested on the flat, muddy beach.

'Well, what next?' asked Algy, as he stepped ashore and moored the amphibian, lightly, in case another hurried departure became necessary.

'We can do nothing but wait here until the petrol comes,' replied Biggles. 'There can't be more than half an hour's supply left in the tanks, and I shall feel a lot happier with a full load on board. Goodness knows when we shall get any more. If he brings more than will go into the tanks, we'll stack it in the cabin. But it's getting Dickpa out that I'm worried about; and that, without knowing a single word of Portuguese—I think that's the lingo they talk here—may be a wee bit difficult. You'll have to stay here and look after the machine,' he went on firmly. 'I'll take Smyth with me on this trip into the town. No! It's no use arguing about it,' he went on quickly. 'I know you'd like to come, and I'd like to have you with me, but you're the only other one of the party who can fly, so you must stay with the machine. If we lose that, we're sunk. After Dickpa, that must be our first consideration. Whatever happens, they mustn't get the *Condor*. Once we've got some juice in the tanks and Dickpa on board, they won't see us for dust and small pebbles. Hark! There's a car coming now. Pass me that 12-bore out of the cabin. I'm taking no chances. They took the first crack at us, and they're going to find that two can play at that game before we're finished.'

The car had stopped quite near them and a dark figure appeared, approaching through the forest belt that lined the shore.

'Is that you, Bigglesworth?' called a voice softly.

'OK, Carter,' replied Biggles. 'Did you get the juice?'

'Yes, it's all here.'

'Good man! Let's see about getting it on board, then. All hands on deck. Smyth, you get the big funnel out and stand by to pour into the tanks while we feed you with the tins. Sling the empties away; we shan't want 'em again.'

For an hour they all toiled with feverish speed and without a break, and at the end of that time the tanks were full and an extra ten tins were stowed in the cabin.

'That's a good job done,' muttered Biggles with satisfaction, mopping his streaming face, for the moist heat on the edge of the tropical forest was intense. 'Are you going straight back to Manaos now, Carter?'

'Yes. I've nothing else to wait here for, unless you want anything.'

'Do you mind if I come with you?'

'Not a bit. Come by all means, although I'm hanged if I can see any way of getting your uncle out. If I can be of any help—'

'You've taken enough risks already,' interrupted Biggles. 'Is there any chance of bribing the guards, do you think?'

'Not a hope. I've tried that already. They're willing enough to accept money, but they're scared stiff of da Silva. If your uncle got away, they'd be for the high jump—and they know it. No, I'm afraid it's force or nothing.'

'Force it is, then,' replied Biggles shortly. 'Come on, Smyth. I may need some help. Algy, you stand by for a quick move.'

He dived into the cabin and emerged with two revolvers and a steel mooring-spike. 'Take this, Smyth,' he said, handing the mechanic one of the revolvers, 'but don't use it unless you have to, and then use the butt for preference. If we kill somebody, the fat will be in the fire with a vengeance. All set? Off we go, then. Cheerio, Algy. Keep your prop on contact.'

A brief handshake and they had climbed aboard the old Ford and were on their way back to Manaos.

Chapter 6
Escape

'Just what do you think you are going to do when you get into the town?' asked Carter as the lights of Manaos shone through the trees ahead.

'I haven't the faintest idea, and that's a fact,' admitted Biggles reluctantly. 'I'm not even trying to make a plan until I've seen the lay-out of the place where they've locked my uncle up.'

'Well, I'd better drop you here, I think,' continued the agent, slowing up. 'They haven't seen you yet—at least, not at close quarters—so they don't know you, which is all to your advantage; but if they see us together they'll form a shrewd idea who you are, and you'll be a marked man.'

'Good enough,' replied Biggles. 'That sounds wise to me. We don't want to involve you in trouble, anyway. How do you get to this place—this Stretta something-or-other?'

'Fontana. Go straight down the avenue which is a continuation of this track, take the third turning on the right, and it's about a hundred yards down on the left. You can't miss it; there's a gendarme on duty at the door.'

'How many guards have they inside, do you think?'

'To tell you the truth, I don't know; probably not more than two or three. As you go in through the door there is an office on the right where the chief officer sits. There's a short corridor leading straight ahead, and the cells are at the end, facing you, at right angles to it. The doors are open, grille-like affairs, like the American prisons,' concluded Carter.

'I see,' answered Biggles, climbing out of the car. 'Just a minute before you go.' He stooped and groped around the axle of the car until his hand was covered with black oil, which he smeared over his face. 'You'd better do the same, Smyth,' he advised; 'we shan't be quite so conspicuous if our faces are a little less white. Well, goodbye, Mr. Carter, in case we don't see you again,' he went on, turning to the agent. 'Many thanks for all you've done. I'll see that my uncle knows about it.'

With a parting wave, he set off with Smyth up the long avenue that opened in front of them. They took the third turning, as directed, passed the cathedral, and pulled up opposite a low building in front of which two gendarmes were idly talking and smoking.

'Well, there it is,' muttered Biggles, half to himself, taking a careful look around to mark his bearings. It was still early, and most of the shops on either side of the street were still lighted. 'This would be easier if we could speak the language,' he went on quietly. 'We had better try and locate the river first, to get a line of retreat in case we have to bolt. We don't want to trail all the way back by that infernal forest track. A boat would be easier. The river should be down here somewhere—yes, here it is,' he continued, as the moonlit river came into view.

There were plenty of small boats by the water's edge, and there appeared to be no obstacle in the way of purloining one. After a cautious look around, Biggles picked out a canoe, and, having satisfied himself that there were paddles in it, he moved it a few yards nearer the water. 'That's the one,' he said quietly. 'If we get separated, make for here. Come on, let's get back.'

Again Biggles regarded the jail from the opposite side of the road. 'If I could speak their beastly language I should try bribing the guards; I've plenty of money on me,' muttered Biggles.

'Well, as we can't, that isn't much use,' observed Smyth shortly.

'You don't often speak, but when you do you say something,' grinned Biggles. 'Stand fast while I have a closer look.'

He walked on a few yards, crossed the road, and then strolled slowly back past the jail. It was a wretched, dilapidated-looking place, like most of the other buildings in the vicinity, and built of adobe, or mud bricks. Through a small window he could see the chief gendarme at his desk, exactly as Carter had described. He retraced his footsteps, and joined Smyth on the opposite side of the road again.

'If we could get everybody out of the building for a couple of minutes it would be simple,' he mused, 'but how to do it—that's the question.'

They strolled a few yards farther on, and suddenly Biggles paused in his stride and nudged Smyth in the ribs. Just beyond the jail was an open yard filled with wooden cases and several piles of dried palm fronds, which were evidently used as packing for the stacks of adobe bricks that stood at the far end of the yard. Biggles eyed it reflectively, and then, followed by Smyth, crossed over to it. A flimsy fence with a gate, which they quickly ascertained was locked, separated the yard from the road. He turned as a car pulled up a short distance away and a man alighted, lit a cigarette, and then disappeared into a private house. Biggles strolled idly towards the car, his eyes running over it swiftly. It was a Ford, and he noted the spare tin of petrol fastened to the running-board.

'I want that tin,' he hissed. 'Get it off while I stand in front to hide you as much as I can.'

It was the work of a moment for Smyth to unscrew the butterfly bolts that held the tin in place.

'Good. This way,' whispered Biggles, and led the way back to the yard. He looked quickly up and down the road. There were one or two pedestrians about, but no one was taking the slightest notice of them. With his jack-knife Biggles unscrewed the metal cap of the petrol-tin and then tossed the whole thing on to the nearest heap of palm fronds. Leaning against the gate, they could hear the steady gurgle of the liquid as it gushed out. 'So far so good,' he muttered softly. 'Now, Smyth, when we move we've got to make it snappy. Speed is everything.' He turned and looked again at the car, which was still standing by the curb. 'I wonder,' he mused. 'I wonder. It would make a good job of the thing,' he went on, half to himself. 'Did you bring your nerve with you, Smyth?'

The old flight-sergeant chuckled. 'Never left it behind yet, sir,' he smiled.

'Have you got enough to drive that car slap through this gate? I want to make a noise, a real bang, the bigger the better. Drive the car straight up the road on the other side, then swerve right across straight through the gate. It's only thin, and will go to pieces like matchwood, so you shouldn't get hurt; I wouldn't suggest it if there was any chance of that. Have a box of matches in your hand, and when you hit that bunch of palm leaves strike one and set the whole works on fire. Then let out a good yell or two and bolt for the canoe. Wait for me there. Have you got that?'

Smyth nodded. 'I have, sir,' he grinned delightedly. 'I've wanted to do something like that all my life.'

'Well, now's your chance,' retorted Biggles brightly; 'go to it.'

He turned on his heel and walked away without another word. Outside the jail he stopped and leaned against a tall palm, as if in contemplation of the starry sky. A couple of yards away a single gendarme squatted on the step in front of the open doors of the jail, and, except for a faint breeze which rustled the leathery palm-tops, all was quiet. One by one the lights in the shops were going out; a few wayfarers were meandering slowly, after the fashion of the tropics, along the street.

Biggles heard a car start up not far away and braced himself for what was to follow, feeling for the mooring-pin under his coat. He heard the car coming nearer and a clash of gears as the driver made a bad change. There was a sudden shout of alarm, and out of the corner of his eye he saw the gendarme spring to his feet. Then came a screeching of skidding wheels and even Biggles, who knew what was coming, was utterly unprepared for the crash that followed. In the sultry calm of the tropic night it sounded like the end of the world. For a fleeting instant there was silence, a silence in which Biggles stood rooted to the ground, too stunned to move. Then a long, piercing yell rent the air.

Biggles turned pale. 'Strewth,' he whispered, 'he must have killed himself.' But there was no time for idle speculation. Pandemonium broke loose. Windows were flung open, dogs barked, doors banged, and there was a great noise of shouting and running feet. A lurid glow, quickly increasing in intensity, illuminated the scene in a ghastly glare.

The gendarme who had been on duty had disappeared at a run at the first crash, and now three or four others, some hatless and others coatless, bundled out of the door and dashed towards the scene of ruin

60

on which a crowd was now converging in a babble of wild excitement. Biggles waited for no more. He swung round on his heel and darted towards the open door, almost colliding with the chief gendarme on the steps. But the official was too taken up with the unusual occurrence to even notice him. With the mooring-spike in his hand, Biggles sprinted down the corridor towards what looked like a row of cages and from which came an excited chatter.

'Dickpa!' he shouted. 'Where are you?'

'Here.'

Biggles leapt towards the iron grille through which Dickpa was peering and dancing with excitement.

'Take it steady,' said Biggles, as cold as ice now the actual action was in progress. Inserting his spike between the grille and the wall, and using the latter as a fulcrum for his lever, he flung his weight behind the instrument.

'Look out!' yelled Dickpa.

Biggles ducked as he turned. Something swished through the air over his head; it was a truncheon wielded by a gigantic policeman. Had the blow, struck with all the power of the man's arm, reached its mark, Biggles's part in the affair would have ended forthwith. As it was, however, the blow spent itself on empty air; the man overbalanced from his own impetus, stumbled, and then pitched headlong over the foot that Biggles had flung out to trip him. The pilot was on him in a flash. His spike descended in a short, gleaming arc that landed on the back of the fallen man's skull. Turning, he whipped out his revolver and thrust it through the bars into Dickpa's hands.

'Use that if you have to,' he said grimly. 'We might as well be hung for sheep as lambs.' He thrust the spike through the bars again and flung his weight on

61

it. The wall crumbled for a moment, and then, with a crash, the lock tore itself through the dry clay wall and the door flew open. 'Come on,' was all he said, and, heedless of the yells and groans from the other prisoners, he raced towards the door with Dickpa at his heels.

As he reached it, he paused for an instant, aghast at the scene that met his eyes. The street was packed solid with people watching the roaring conflagration that seemed to reach half way to the sky. 'Strewth,' he gasped, 'I've heard of people setting a town alight, but we seem to have done it. Come on, hang on to my coat; if we lose each other we're sunk. Keep your face down or someone may recognize you.'

Jostling, pushing, and snarling, they forced their way through the throng and hurried towards the river. A shrill whistle split the air from the direction of the jail.

'They've missed you,' muttered Biggles grimly. 'No matter, we shall take some catching now.'

'Where are you making for?' gasped Dickpa.

'The river,' replied Biggles tersely. 'Follow me, and don't talk,' he added, with an excusable lack of respect. 'Here we are,' he went on, as they reached the rendezvous. 'Hullo!' He pulled up with a jerk. The boat had gone.

'Here you are, sir,' called a voice from the darkness a few yards ahead.

'Good man, Smyth,' cried Biggles, as he saw the faint outline of the mechanic in the canoe, already on the water. 'In you go, Dickpa.'

Obediently Dickpa stepped aboard, and settled himself on the floor with a sigh of relief. 'Where's the machine?' he asked calmly.

'A bit lower down the river—Algy is in charge.'

'Good.'

Biggles picked up a paddle, and with a quick shove sent the canoe far out into the stream. 'Straight ahead, Smyth,' he muttered as he drove his paddle into the water. 'I don't think there is any immediate cause for alarm, but the sooner we get to the machine the better. They won't know which way we've gone, that's one good thing.'

Ten minutes brisk paddling brought them to the creek where the amphibian glowed dully white in the moonlight.

'Algy, ahoy!' hailed Biggles.

'Got him?' came Algy's voice over the water.

'Yes, we're all here,' cried Dickpa gaily.

'Fine,' answered Algy, with intense satisfaction.

They climbed aboard and kicked the boat adrift.

'What's the next move?' asked Dickpa with some concern. 'They'll hunt the river upstream and down-stream before morning, looking for us.'

'Well, I'm not going to take off before dawn unless I'm compelled to,' replied Biggles. 'We'll cut loose and drift out into midstream, from where we shall see anyone coming as soon as they see us. We shall have to take it in turns to keep watch. Let her go, Algy.'

Chapter 7
The Falls

The rays of the rising sun were tingeing the tree-tops with gold and orange as the amphibian, with her engine purring like a well-oiled sewing-machine, swung round in a circle to face the stream in readiness for a take-off.

'It's about time we went,' muttered Biggles to Dickpa, who sat beside him in order to act as guide, and nodded towards a distant bend in the river, around which a launch came into view, two feathers of spray flying back from her bows betraying the urgency of her mission, which was made still more apparent by a group of uniformed men crowding near the bows. 'Well, boys, it's too bad, but you're just too late,' he murmured with mock sympathy as he opened the throttle.

The purr of the engine rose to a deep, vibrating roar that sent a cloud of macaws wheeling and screeching into the air from the trees on the bank. The *Condor* moved forward with swiftly increasing speed, and, after a quick glance at the instrument-board to make sure the engine was giving her full revolutions, the pilot drew the joystick back towards his safety belt. The amphibian left the water like a gull and rose gracefully into the air.

Slowly the tropic sun swung upwards into a sky no longer turquoise, but hard steely blue. Its rays struck full upon the polished hull of the amphibian and flashed from time to time in glittering points of light on the goggles of the pilot as he moved his head to scan the

64

savage panorama below. Manaos, shining whitely, soon lay far astern.

For two hours they cruised steadily westwards, following the winding river that wound like a silver snake to the far horizon. From time to time they passed over places where the river assumed a milky whiteness, and Biggles hardly needed Dickpa to tell him that such stretches indicated foaming rapids where the water hurled itself over boulders as it dropped swiftly to the lower level. Occasionally the river disappeared under filmy clouds of spray where it dropped over gigantic falls into boiling whirlpools below. On each side lay the vast, untrodden, primæval forest, dark and forbidding, hiding the earth under an unpenetrable canopy of mystery. Biggles, as he watched it, could not help reflecting on the strange fascination that urged men like Dickpa to leave home, comfort, and security to face its hidden terrors.

He was aroused from his reverie by a light touch on the arm, and turned sharply, to find Dickpa pointing at something ahead upon which he had riveted his gaze. Following the outstretched finger, he saw a wide tributary branching away to the south, and with a sharp inclination of his thumb Dickpa indicated that he was to follow it.

In spite of his habitual coolness, Biggles felt a thrill of excitement run through him. Before them, not far away, lay something which a thousand men had sought in vain, and presently, all being well, it would be his good fortune to see it. Treasure! The very word, charged with the romance of ages, was sufficient to bring a sparkle to the eyes.

Obediently he swung round in a gentle bank to follow the new river. For another half-hour he flew on, once exchanging a grim smile with Dickpa as they passed a foaming cascade. The forest on each side began to give way slowly to more open country, and presently they could see vast stretches of rolling prairie spreading into the far distance.

Biggles suddenly caught his breath as the note of the engine changed. It was slight, so slight that only a pilot or an engineer would have noticed it; he did not move a muscle, but listened intently to the almost imperceptible hesitation in the regular rhythm. Then, without further warning, the engine cut out dead. Before the whirling propeller had run to a standstill Biggles had pushed his joystick forward and was going down in a long, gentle glide towards the river, eyes searching swiftly for the best landing-place.

After the first start of surprise when the engine had so unexpectedly stopped, Dickpa remained perfectly still, watching the pilot for any signal he might make. Once, as Biggles glanced in his direction, his lips formed the word 'Parachute,' but the pilot shook his head severely. The details of the river grew clearer. A long, straight reach lay before them, and Biggles, losing height steadily, headed the amphibian towards it.

With his lips set in a straight line, he glued his eyes on the water for signs of rocks or other obstructions which might rip the bottom out of the delicate hull, but he relaxed with relief when he saw all was clear.

Swish . . . swish . . . swish . . . sang the keel, as it kissed the placid water, and a moment later it had settled down as it ran to a stop in the middle of the stream.

'Confound it!' snapped Biggles irritably, his voice sounding strangely unnatural in the silence.

'What is it, do you think—anything serious?' asked Dickpa anxiously.

'No, I shouldn't think so,' replied Biggles.

'Sounded like magneto to me, sir, the way she cut out so sudden like,' observed Smyth, climbing into the cockpit and then out on to the hull behind the engine. 'I shall have to wait a minute or two to let her cool down before I can do anything,' he added.

'Well, there doesn't appear to be any particular hurry,' said Biggles. 'We were lucky she cut out where she did and not somewhere over the forest or one of those places where the river wound about so much. Have a look at her, Smyth, and tell me if you want any help.'

For a quarter of an hour or twenty minutes Smyth laboured at the engine, the others watching him with interest. 'It's the mag, as I thought,' remarked the mechanic; 'brush has gone. I've a spare, inside.'

In a few minutes the faulty part was replaced and the cause of the breakdown remedied. As Smyth reached for the magneto cover, and a spanner to bolt it on, Biggles turned away casually to return to his cockpit, but the next moment a shrill cry of alarm broke from his lips as he pointed to the bank, past which they were floating with ever-increasing speed.

'We've drifted to the head of some rapids,' said Dickpa crisply. 'Get the engine started; we've no time to lose.'

An eddy caught the nose of the *Condor* and spun the machine round on its own length. They swung dizzily round a bend, and as the new vista came into view a cry of horror broke from Algy, and he pointed, white faced. High in the air, not a quarter of a mile away, hung a great white cloud. A low rumble, like the roll of distant thunder rapidly approaching, reached the ears of the listeners.

'The falls!' cried Biggles. 'The falls! Get that mag

jacket on, Smyth, for heaven's sake; if it isn't on in two minutes we're lost.'

The current had now seized the machine in its relentless grip and was whirling it along at terrific speed; from time to time an eddy would swing it round dizzily, a manœuvre the pilot had no means of checking.

'Look out!' Algy, taking his life in his hands, reached far over the side and fended the *Condor* away from a jagged point of rock that thrust a black, tooth-like spur above the surface. By his presence of mind the danger was averted almost before it had arisen, but little flecks of foam marked the positions of more ahead. Straight across their path lay a long, black boulder, a miniature island around which the water seethed and raged in white, lashed fury.

'If we hit that, we're sunk,' snapped Biggles. 'How long will you be, Smyth?'

'One minute, sir.'

'That's thirty seconds too long,' replied Biggles, and the truth of his words was only too apparent to the others, for the *Condor* was literally racing towards the rock as if determined to destroy herself. A bare hundred yards beyond it the river ended abruptly where it plunged out of sight into the mighty, seething cauldron below. The rock seemed to literally leap towards them.

'Steady, Algy! Leave me if I don't make the bank,' barked Biggles, and before the others could realize his intention, he had seized a mooring-rope and taken a flying leap onto the rock. He landed on his feet and flung his weight against the nose of the machine. Waterborne, it swung away swiftly. The tail whipped round, the elevators literally grazing the rock, and the next instant it was clear. Biggles took a lightning turn of the rope round a jutting piece of rock and flung himself backward to take the strain:

The rope jerked taut with a twang like a great banjo-string, and the *Condor*, nose towards the rock, remained motionless, two curling feathers of spray leaping up from her bow as it cut the raging torrent. Algy, in the cockpit, was winding the self-starter furiously, and looked up as the engine came to life. He opened the throttle, and the machine began to surge slowly towards the rock. For a minute Biggles watched it uncomprehendingly. The rope was slack and the engine was roaring on full throttle, yet the *Condor* was making little or no headway. It seemed absurd, but as the truth became obvious his heart grew cold with horror. Slowly the full significance of what was happening dawned upon him. He realised that against the rapids it was an utter impossibility for the machine to make sufficient headway to get enough flying speed to lift it. They were in the middle of the stream, and to attempt to reach either bank would mean they would inevitably go sideways over the falls before they could reach it. Only one path remained—downstream—and that way lay the falls. For a moment or two Biggles did not even consider it, but then, as he saw it was the only way they *could* go unless they intended to remain for ever as they were, he began to weigh up the chances.

There was no wind. The current was running at perhaps thirty or forty miles an hour, and that would consequently be the *Condor*'s speed the instant she was released. Another twenty or thirty miles an hour on top of that and they would be travelling at nearly seventy miles an hour, which was ample for a take-off. The only doubt in his mind was whether or not she would 'unstick.' He knew, of course, that nearly all marine aircraft were slow to leave the water unless they got a 'kick' from a wave or the assistance of broken water. That was a risk he would have to take, he decided.

The *Condor*, still under full throttle, had nearly nosed up to the rock now, and Biggles saw that Algy was shouting. He could not hear what he said for the noise of the engine and the rushing water, but he could guess by his actions what he was trying to convey. Algy was trying to tell him that the machine could not get sufficient flying speed to rise against such a current. 'I know that,' thought Biggles grimly as he examined the course he would have to take as he went downstream. There were several rocks projecting above the water, but fortunately none in a direct line between him and the falls.

The *Condor* was just holding its own against the current, travelling so slowly that it would require far more petrol than they had on board for it to ever get above the rapids. Biggles made up his mind suddenly, and sprang like a cat for the nose of the machine. He jerked down into his seat while Algy stared at him with ashen face. Biggles motioned him into his seat, reached over, and cut the rope and then kicked the rudder hard over. The *Condor* bucked like a wild horse as the stream caught her, and the next instant they were tearing through a sea of spray towards apparent destruction.

Eighty yards—seventy—sixty—Biggles bit his lip. Would she never lift? The combined noise of the engine and the falls was devastating, yet the pilot did not swerve an inch. Thirty yards from the bank he glanced at his air speed indicator, and then jerked the stick back into his stomach. The machine lifted, hung for a moment as if undecided as to whether to go on or fall back on the water again, then picked up and plunged into the opaque cloud of spray.

The pilot's heart missed a beat as they rocked

and dropped like a stone in the terrific 'bump,' or down current, caused by the cold, moisture-soaked atmosphere. The engine spluttered, missed fire, picked up again, missed, and Biggles thought the end had come. He knew only too well the cause of the trouble; the spray was pouring into the air intake and choking his engine.*

The *Condor* burst out into the sunshine on the other side of the cloud, the engine picked up with a shrill crescendo bellow, and the machine soared upward like a bird. Out of the corner of his eye Biggles caught a glimpse of the rocktorn maelstrom below, and leaned back limply in his cockpit. He caught Algy's eye and shook his head weakly, as if the matter was beyond words. Algy gave him a sickly grin and disappeared into the cabin, to allow Dickpa to resume his seat in the cockpit in order to point out the way.

Dickpa leaned towards him. 'I thought you said this was the safest form of transport in the world!' he bellowed** sarcastically.

'Quite right,' yelled Biggles. 'Where would you have been in a canoe?'

Dickpa shook his head with a wry face and turned his attention to the ground below. They had already passed the place where they had come down on the water and were nearing the open prairies ahead. Tall trees, chiefly buriti palms, and thick vegetation lined the riverbanks, but Biggles saw several places where a landing might be safely attempted. Mountain ranges

* When Biggles was telling me about this particular incident I reminded him that Sir Alan Cobham once had a similar narrow escape from the same cause whilst flying over the Victoria Falls on one of his African flights of survey.
** Normal speech would be impossible with an open cockpit due to the noise of the engine and the rush of air.

appeared at several points in the distance, their blue tints, caused by the clear atmosphere, giving way to a dull red colour as they drew nearer.

Biggles was amazed at the grotesque formation of the rocks. Against the skyline they often looked, as Dickpa had said, like mighty frowning castles, complete with battlements and turrets, but at close quarters the resemblance was lost in a maze of pinnacles, gaunt, stark, and utterly desolate. He was staring at a startling pile of rock, blood-red with yellow ochre streaks, when Dickpa touched him on the arm and pointed downwards. Biggles looked, and saw that in one or two places where the river skirted the foot of the mountains it widened out into a sort of lagoon. Turning, he raised his eyebrows enquiringly, and, in answer to Dickpa's signal, throttled back and began a long spiral glide towards the largest stretch of water. The landing presented no difficulties, and the *Condor* soon ran to a standstill on the smooth water. Biggles taxied up to the bank, switched off, and, as the engine fitfully spluttered to silence, raised himself stiffly and looked around.

'Well, here we are,' said Dickpa brightly. 'I think this is the safest place where we could land within a striking distance of the actual spot for which we are bound. It is still a little distance away, but within walking distance, so there seems to be no need to risk a landing on hard ground.'

Biggles surveyed the place with interest. Seen from water-level, they appeared to be on a lake, enclosed on three sides by a wall of dark green foliage, and on the other by an awe-inspiring mass of rock that rose, tier by tier, far into the blue sky above. This was the side towards which Biggles had taxied, for a narrow strip of shelving sand fringed the river and formed a small beach on which they could step ashore. Near at hand

72

a mass of exotic flowers overran some low bushes and fell in a vivid scarlet cascade to the very edge of the water. A humming-bird darted towards the *Condor*, hung poised for a moment on vibrating wings, and then flashed like a living jewel towards the flowers. A flight of blue and orange macaws passed overhead, uttering harsh metallic cries, and Biggles turned towards Dickpa with an appreciative smile.

'Nice spot,' he observed cheerfully.

'It looks like it,' agreed Dickpa quietly, 'but things are not always what they seem in this part of the world. Take a look at that fellow, for instance,' he added, pointing.

The others followed the finger with their eyes, and were just in time to see a long, dark shadow glide into the water.

'What a horror!' muttered Biggles with a shudder.

'Anaconda—quite harmless,' returned Dickpa calmly. 'It's the little fellows that do the damage. Comparatively few snakes are venomous, really deadly, but it takes some time to learn which they are. The safest thing is to keep clear of all of them.'

'You needn't tell me that,' replied Biggles warmly. 'I shan't worry them if they don't worry me. What is our plan now?' he enquired, changing the subject.

'I don't think we can do better than make camp here,' answered Dickpa. 'We'll moor the machine securely, so that she can't drift away, and then get some stores out. We'll go on foot to the treasure-cave tomorrow. It's only a few miles away, but I am afraid it's too late for us to start today; this is no place to be benighted, as you may learn before we're finished.'

'That suits me,' agreed Biggles. 'Smyth had better have a good look over the machine. There isn't very much to do here, don't you think it would be a good idea if I took a stroll along the river-bank and made a rough survey for shoals or rocks, in case there are any about? We might have to take off in a hurry, and it's as well to be on the safe side.'

'Very wise,' replied Dickpa at once. 'There might be an old tree-trunk or two on the water and we don't want to hit anything like that, I imagine.'

'We certainly do not,' returned Biggles emphatically.

'All right, you take a look around while Algy and I get the hammocks ashore. By the way, I should take a gun with you.'

'I'm not likely to go without one,' grinned Biggles. 'I haven't forgotten the gentleman we just saw slithering into the water.'

'Oh, he won't worry you, but mind you don't step on a croc, and don't eat any fruit without showing it to me first,' was Dickpa's final warning as Biggles, with an Express rifle under his arm, set off up the river.

Chapter 8
Indians

While the beach lasted, Biggles found the going easy, but he advanced cautiously, keeping a watchful eye on the bushes that skirted the foot of the cliff; presently large boulders and rocks that had fallen from above obstructed his path, and progress became slower. From time to time he climbed up to the top of these and examined the surface of the water critically; he was soon glad that he had taken the precaution, for in many places he could see great masses of dark rock just below the surface which would have crushed the bottom of the *Condor* like an eggshell, had the amphibian come in contact with them when taking off.

The position of these he tried to memorise, and, to make doubly sure, he marked them down on a rough sketch-map. From time to time he could still see the machine, with its nose almost touching the beach, and the others carrying things from it to the shore, but now the bank curved inwards and hid them from view. A swarm of insects began to collect above him, and he struck savagely at the bees that settled and clung persistently to his face. 'What a curse you are!' he growled as he quickly discovered that his efforts were unrewarded.

The sun, now past its zenith, was blazing hot, and the going became still more difficult. Great trees, festooned with lianas, began to crowd down to the water's edge, and he advanced more warily. Once a butterfly, with wings as large as the palms of his hands, brought his heart into his mouth as it darted within a foot of his face in swift, bird-like flight.

In the shade of the trees the heat was even more oppressive, and the silence uncanny. When he stood still he could hear furtive rustlings among the dead leaves at his feet and all around him, and these, he ascertained by careful investigation, were caused by ants as they toiled indefatigably at innumerable tasks. Once he halted to watch an incredible army of them passing by, marching steadily in a long, winding column that disappeared into the dim recesses of the jungle.

Turning another corner, he pulled up dead in his tracks and slowly brought his rifle to the ready. Straight in front of him, near the water's edge, and not fifty yards away, was a palm-thatched shack in the last stages of dilapidation. Near it was a canoe, also very much the worse for wear, with a paddle lying across it.

'Anyone at home?' he called loudly.

All remained silent except for the buzzing of the countless insects.

He approached warily. 'Anyone at home?' he called again, eyeing the canoe suspiciously. 'If the occupant is not inside, how has he departed without his canoe, his only means of transport?' he mused. As he drew closer he saw that a tangle of weeds had sprung up inside the boat, and it was evident that it had not been moved for some time. With a grim suspicion already half formed in his mind, he was not altogether surprised at what he saw when he pushed the ramshackle door open.

A cloud of flies arose with a loud buzz from an object that lay upon a rough mattress in a corner of the room. He walked slowly over to it, and then turned quickly away. Upon the primitive bed lay what had once been the body of a man—a negro, judging by the short, curly black hair. An old-fashioned muzzle-loading rifle lay beside him, and near it, a glass bottle that had once, according to the label, contained quinine, told its own story. On the far side of the room were a number of rough, round, smoke-blackened balls, about the size of footballs, the product of nature to collect which the man had sacrificed his life.

Biggles knew without examining them closer that they were rubber—the crude, heat-solidified latex of the tree that gave it its name. The gruesome tragedy was plain enough to see. The man had been a rubber collector, and, overtaken with the inevitable fever, had taken to his bed, where, far from the help of others of his kind, he had died a lonely and pitiful death.

Depressed by the sad spectacle, Biggles hastened into the fresh air and looked moodily at the unfortunate man's equipment, and then, with a sigh, passed on, strangely moved by the silent drama of loneliness and death.

But he did not go far. Having achieved the object of his walk, he began to retrace his steps—slowly, for there were many things to interest him. Once it was a spray of orchids that sprang from a rotten tree and which would have cost a small fortune in a London florist's. Sometimes it was a bird of unbelievable colours or shoals of fish in the water. The sun was now low in the sky, and, realising that he had taken longer over his journey than the object of it justified, he quickened his steps.

He reached the beach and breathed a sigh of relief as his eyes picked out the amphibian still at its moorings. Why he was relieved he hardly knew, unless it was that the loneliness of the forest had depressed him.

He could not see the others, but he did not worry on that score; no doubt they were lying in the shade, resting after their efforts. But as he approached and they still did not appear, an unaccountable fear assailed him, although he ridiculed himself for his alarm.

'Ahoy there!' he cried in a ringing, high-pitched voice that reflected his anxiety. There was no reply. The words had echoed to silence before he moved, and then he acted swiftly. He cocked his rifle and, after a quick, penetrating glance around, broke into a swerving run towards the *Condor*. Reaching it, he pulled up in consternation at the sight that met his gaze.

The machine was apparently untouched, yet all around on the beach the sand was kicked up and ploughed in such a way as could only have been caused by a fierce struggle. 'But what? What could they struggle with in such a place?' was the thought that hammered through his brain.

A fire was still smouldering on some stones, and the hammocks, looking as if they had been carelessly flung down, lay near it. Then his eye caught something on the machine that sent him hurrying towards it, ashen faced. It was an arrow, feathered with scarlet macaw pinions.

Indians! So that was it. What had happened he could only guess, but for one thing at least he was thankful. There were no bodies on the beach, and this suggested that Dickpa and the others had been surprised and overpowered before they could reach the weapons in the machine.

'The Indians have got 'em, no doubt of that,' he thought grimly. 'Well, if I can't get them back they may as well have me too. The question is, which way have they gone?' It was easily answered, for an unmistakable track of bare feet led to a flaw in the rock which opened out into a distant path. A few yards farther on he stooped and picked up a tiny white seed with a grunt of satisfaction. Presently he found another, and another. It was rice, and the solution flashed upon him at once.

The Indians had seized the stores that had been taken ashore, and among them was a bag of rice. Luckily the bag had a hole in it, or perhaps—remembering what Dickpa had told them in England—an ant had already started its nefarious work while the bag was lying on the beach. At any rate, unless the Indian carrying the bag discovered the leak, he was leaving a trail that should not be difficult to follow.

How long had they been gone? He did not know and had no means of telling. He glanced at the sun, now almost touching the horizon. 'It will be dark in half an hour, I've no time to lose,' he muttered. Weapons! He was still carrying the Express, but would that be enough? 'I might as well have a revolver for close work,' he thought, and dashed back to the *Condor*.

He opened the locker where the small arms were kept, and, selecting an automatic, with half a dozen spare clips of ammunition, slipped them into his pocket. He was about to drop the lid on the locker when his eye lighted on something that made him pause. 'That might be useful,' he thought quickly, and added a squat Véry pistol, used for signalling purposes, to his collection. He grabbed a couple of handfuls of cartridges at random and, after a final look around to see that the *Condor* was securely moored, set off at a quick pace on the trail of the Indians.

The path became more difficult as he advanced, and he was glad when it swung round away from the mountains, plunged through a ravine, and then came out on the rolling *matto*, or open plain dotted with groups of shrubs and trees. He picked up a button, and recognized it at once as one from Algy's coat. Presently he found another, and then a stub of lead pencil, and guessed that Algy was deliberately discarding such small things as he was able, to mark the trail for him, knowing that the Indians were unaware of his existence.

The heat was terrific, and his face streamed with perspiration—a matter the insects seemed to appreciate, for they nearly drove him distracted with their unwelcome attentions. A hundred times he remembered Dickpa's words about the bees that clung to his nose, ears, and eyes with their hooked feet. He looked behind him continually, not so much for possible enemies as to mark the configuration of the trees and rocks against the skyline, to guide him on his return journey—if there was to be one.

He came upon the Indian camp suddenly, and all else was at once forgotten. It was built on the bank of a brook which he thought might be a tributary of the larger river on which the *Condor* was moored. He could see several figures moving about, but, as far as he could discover, no guards or sentries were posted. The village consisted simply of a circle of reed-thatched huts from which, even as he watched, a crowd of thirty or forty Indians poured out in wild excitement.

Dropping to his hands and knees, he crawled nearer, regardless of the ants that bit and stung him all over. It was now nearly dark, and the details of the scene were hard to distinguish, but presently a fire was lighted in the centre of the village, and by its bright flickering light he could see everything perfectly. Darkness fell, and he crawled nearer until he was not more than thirty yards away, crouching on the edge of a thick patch of native corn.

He caught his breath as Dickpa, Algy, and Smyth were led out of a hut and dragged towards a row of stakes that stood near the fire.

'Well, it's now or never,' muttered Biggles through his teeth. Holding the rifle under his left arm, he loaded the Véry pistol and placed a relay of cartridges on the ground in front of him. Pointing the muzzle high into the air above the Indians, he pulled the trigger. At the crash of the explosion they stood stock still in petrified astonishment; then, as the flare, which happened to be red, burst with a second explosion immediately over their heads and flooded the scene with crimson radiance, such a pandemonium of screams and yells broke out that even Biggles was startled. But he did not hesitate.

Bang! Bang! Bang! Loading and firing as swiftly as he could, he sent a shower of blazing meteors over the heads of the now panic-stricken Indians. Green, yellow, red, and white, the signal flares filled the air and drenched the village in a ghastly multi-coloured blaze of light. One of them fell upon the roof of a hut, which, tinder dry, at once burst into flames and added further to the inferno. His last cartridge fired, Biggles thrust the weapon in his pocket, and, with the automatic in one hand and rifle in the other, he charged, yelling with all the power of his lungs.

It was the last straw. The Indians, already demoralized, scattered in all directions, shouting, falling, and crashing into the forest. One of them rushed blindly in Biggles's direction, but twisted like a hare and darted away as the automatic exploded.

'Are you all right?' gasped Biggles as he reached Dickpa's side.

'Yes, but my hands are tied.'

Biggles whipped out his jack-knife and quickly

slashed through the lianas that bound his uncle's hands. 'Watch out,' he said shortly, handing him the rifle. In a few seconds the others were freed, and without another word they set off in single file at a sharp trot over the way they had come.

'All right, easy all,' gasped Biggles when they had covered a couple of hundred yards. 'We don't want to get lost in this stuff.' He jabbed his thumb towards the thick *matto* on either side. 'By the way, is anybody hurt? Good,' he ejaculated, in answer to the swift replies in the negative; 'then we should soon be back. I'll go first, because I know the way. Algy, you come next; then you, Smyth; Dickpa, will you bring up the rear with the rifle? If you hear anybody following us, pass the word along. Come on, quick march.'

Across the silent *matto* they hurried, Biggles once pulling up short as a long feline body crossed their path just in front and disappeared into the bushes with a coughing grunt.

'Jaguar—watch out!' called Dickpa from the rear.

Biggles made no reply, but pressed forward, the others close behind, stumbling over rocks and uneven surfaces when they reached the ravine. Slipping and sliding, with many a sharp exclamation of pain as they knocked their shins, they scrambled down the final declivity to the beach where the amphibian was moored.

'Hark!' It was Dickpa who spoke. He stood with his head bent in a listening position. 'They're coming,' he went on. 'We'd better get aboard.'

'I daren't risk taking off in this light,' said Biggles sharply.

'No need to,' replied Dickpa. 'We shall have to get away from the shore, though. It doesn't matter if we do drift downstream a bit; there are no rapids up here.

I know this stretch of water. It was not far from here that my porters absconded. Lend me that jack-knife of yours.'

Biggles handed over the instrument and Dickpa disappeared into the darkness. There was a sudden crashing in the bushes, and he returned a few moments later with three or four long bamboo poles. 'We can keep the machine straight with these,' he said. 'The water isn't very deep, so we can content ourselves with punting—and we'd better be quick about it,' he added, as a series of yells broke out not far away in the direction from which they had come.

The hammocks and the few things that had been taken ashore were hastily flung aboard, and in a few seconds, by the aid of their improvised punt-poles, they were sailing smoothly with the current on the broad face of the river.

The moon rose and flooded the river with a silvery radiance that only served to intensify the blackness of the forest walls on either side.

'We'll go right across to the other side,' announced Dickpa presently. 'The Indians can't have any canoes about, so we shall be quite safe, and I think I remember a useful sort of backwater a bit lower down.'

'Let's go then, by all means,' replied Biggles quickly. 'A bite of food seems indicated,' he added in a complaining tone of voice.

'You wait until you've been ten days without any, as I have,' rejoined Dickpa.

'I trust we shan't come to that,' answered Biggles gloomily. 'I've only had one day of it so far, but I begin to see that this tropical exploring business has its drawbacks. These confounded mosquitoes are pretty awful, aren't they?'

'Bah! That's nothing,' grinned Dickpa. 'You wait until we get to the bank; there'll be more there.'

Biggles groaned. 'Well, let's know the worst,' he growled. 'Is this the place you had in mind?'

'Yes, this is it,' returned Dickpa.

'Then I don't think much of it,' muttered Biggles, with a sudden shiver in spite of the heat. 'It gives me the creeps—reminds me of what I saw up the river—'

'What did you see?' asked Algy curiously.

'Oh, nothing,' replied Biggles shortly, preferring not to go into details in such a place as the one in which they now found themselves.

The *Condor*, like a vague spectral shape, floated on a pool of water as black and motionless as pitch. Completely encircling them except for the narrow opening where they had entered, a wall of black mangroves raised themselves on twisted stilt-like legs, as motionless as if they had been carved in ebony.

Long snake-like lianas hung down to the water. In one place only there was a narrow strip of mud, and, behind it, a small open space where for some unknown reason the living forest had failed to secure a foothold.

'I'm all for staying on the boat,' observed Biggles. 'I never saw such a place in my life; it fairly gives me the creeps. What the dickens are you doing, Smyth?' he went on angrily. 'Don't rock the boat like that. I nearly went overboard.'

'I didn't rock the boat, sir,' came Smyth's startled voice from the darkness at the other end of the machine.

'What th—Hi! Hold on!' Biggles's voice rose sharply as some unseen hand seemed to lift the machine half out of the water. Something hard and scaly scraped along the keel; ripples, long, black, and oily, began to creep across the sullen water. 'What is it, Dickpa?' called Biggles in a startled voice.

A stab of brilliant flame and the thundering roar of an explosion shattered the silence. It was followed by a deep choking cough, and something long and vague began threshing in the water beside them. Other similar shapes flung themselves upon it, and instantly the water became a churning mass of foam and writhing bodies. Something crashed against the hull, making the *Condor* shiver from stem to stern.

'Crocs!' snapped Dickpa. 'The water's full of them. Had to shoot—one was trying to climb up on the tail. Get that engine going and let's get ashore; they'll knock the machine to pieces at this rate.'

The others needed no second invitation; indeed, the necessity for instant action was apparent. Hard, heavy bodies were striking the machine with a force that threatened to shatter it. The self-starter whirred, the engine came to life, the machine skimmed across the water, and, as Biggles dropped his wheels, nosed up on the muddy beach. 'Keep going, Algy!' he cried, handing over the joystick and jumping ashore. 'Keep her straight—that's all right, you've plenty of room. Fine. You'll do. Come on, let's get a fire going.'

Dickpa joined him, a can of petrol in his hand, and a blazing fire soon revealed their white and startled faces.

'What sort of place do you call this, Dickpa?' almost snarled Biggles, thoroughly shaken. 'I thought you said you knew a *good* place! I should be sorry to see what you called a bad one. This river is about the limit—horrors, horrors everywhere.'

Dickpa laughed. 'I believe I warned you that the trip wouldn't be a picnic,' he said.

'And, by Jingo, you weren't far wrong,' conceded Biggles.

The machine was hauled up clear of the bank and

the engine shut off. Again the uncanny silence settled upon the forest.

'Even the trees remind me of monsters about to spring,' declared Algy.

'Let's talk about something else, before the place gets on my nerves,' muttered Biggles harshly as they unloaded some stores from the machine. 'How did those Indians get hold of you?'

Around the camp fire, and over a satisfying meal, the story of the Indian raid was told.

'I didn't hear a sound until Dickpa yelled,' admitted Algy. 'You'd been gone the best part of an hour,' he went on, turning to Biggles, 'and I had just looked along the beach to see if you were coming back when I heard a crash and a shout. I whipped round just as a mob of Indians jumped on me. I couldn't do anything; just went down with a bang, with the whole lot of 'em piled on top of me. I kicked and struggled, but it was no use; one man can't fight a crowd. They dragged me to my feet in a sort of a daze, and the first thing I saw was Dickpa and Smyth in the same plight as myself. I still don't know how they got hold of Smyth, because he was on board when they attacked.'

'I was in the cabin unpacking some cases when I heard a shout,' explained Smyth. 'It didn't alarm me much, but I went up on deck to see what it was about, and the first thing I knew was an arrow flitting past my ear.'

'That's right; I saw it. In fact, that's how I knew it was Indians,' confirmed Biggles.

'It looked like a rugger scrum on the beach,' resumed Smyth, 'so I joined in. In my surprise I forgot all about the guns in the cabin—not that they would have been much good. The game was a bit too one-sided, though, and a big chap landed me one with a thing like a coconut on the end of a stick.' The ex-flight-sergeant felt the back of his head gingerly. 'I've a bump there as big as a hen's egg,' he concluded.

'And that's about all there is to tell,' said Dickpa. 'They must have been stalking us for a long time, which shows the folly of not keeping a strict watch all the time when you are in a country like this. Out of the corner of my eye I saw something move, and I looked up just as they broke cover. I let out a yell to try and warn the others, but it was too late. However, all's well that ends well. That was a smart idea of yours, Biggles, using the Véry pistol. Those flares put the wind up them more effectively than anything else could have done. They've never seen such things before; in fact, I very much doubt if they've ever heard a gun go off. They're getting over their fright by this time, and are probably thirsting for our blood. If you hadn't taken that stroll along the beach we should all have been nabbed, and then we should have been in a pretty mess.'

'In the soup, all right,' grinned Biggles.

'Well, we do at least know they're about, that's one thing,' said Dickpa. 'I didn't think they came as far south as this, but of course you can never really tell with these people. I am thankful they were too scared of the machine to go near it. Anyway, they are not likely to follow us here; they're scared stiff of the dark. And now we had better get some sleep; we've got a hard day in front of us tomorrow.'

Chapter 9
A Night of Horror

'Well, what's the plan?' asked Biggles the following morning as he ripped the top off a tin of bully beef for breakfast.

'I think we'll push straight along on foot for the cave; we are on the right side of the river for it,' replied Dickpa. 'We've only about a quarter of a mile of forest to get through and then we come out on to the *matto*. I don't think we can be more than seven or eight miles from the cave at most, and we could do that in three of four hours. That should give us time to break down the wall and get back again before nightfall. The first thing we've got to do is to find out what is behind the wall. If there's nothing, well, we just go home again, that's all. If we strike lucky, we shall have to make our plans according to what we find to bring away. I think the machine will be quite safe here; we couldn't find a better hiding place.'

'Good enough,' replied Biggles. 'Then the sooner we get away the better.'

Dawn, the impressive colourful dawn of the Amazon, was just breaking. Within half an hour loads had been made up, tasks allotted, and the entire party moved off in single file. Smyth, armed with a heavy knife for cutting a way through the undergrowth, took the lead, followed by Dickpa with a compass to keep him straight, knowing full well the danger of wandering from a direct course with such a restricted outlook. He also carried a 12-bore shot-gun under his arm. Algy came next with a fairly heavy load of tools and stores they knew they would require, and Biggles, with another load and the Express rifle, brought up the rear.

The going was not so bad as they expected. Lianas, it is true, had to be cut to form a path through the trackless forest, and detours often had to be made round great fallen trees which from time to time impeded their progress, but in a trifle under an hour they emerged into the open *matto*, proving that Dickpa's calculations had not been far wrong. In the near distance a great range of mountains lifted its gaunt peaks high into the sky.

Progress was now much faster, and when they halted for their third rest, Dickpa announced that they were quite close to the stream up which he had wandered on the day of his discovery of the Inca rock carving, and not more than two miles from the cave itself. The insects caused them great inconvenience, frequent stops having to be made to remove persistent *carrapatos* from one or the other of them. Their faces, too, were soon covered with tiny black spots of congealed blood where these and other pests had left their marks. Nevertheless, they were in good spirits, for it seemed that nothing could now prevent the successful exploration of the cave.

They reached the stream, and paused for a moment to refresh themselves and splash their steaming faces, and then pushed on, wading knee deep in the fresh, clear water. Dickpa, old experienced traveller that he was, was obviously as excited as any of them now that they were so near their goal.

'Round the next corner,' he cried cheerfully, 'and there we are.'

Panting from the heat and their exertions, they hurried round the next bend, which brought them face to face with a dull red cliff that rose in a sheer wall to a tremendous altitude. Dickpa, who had now taken the lead, suddenly began to slow up, at the same time staring at the rock with a puzzled expression on his face. Biggles noticed that he had turned a trifle pale under his tan.

'Funny,' he heard him whisper to himself, 'that's funny; I could have sworn this was the place.' And then, 'It is,' he went on, 'but—'

He turned to the others apologetically. 'Something has gone wrong here,' he said shortly. 'I can't quite see what it is, but I don't think it's anything to worry about. Ah, yes, I see. There's been a slight fall of rock which has buried the mouth of the cave. I'm afraid it's going to give us a bit of work, and it will take a bit of time to clear it. This is the place, there's no doubt of that.'

'Well, we can't help it,' said Biggles quickly, feeling more sorry about his uncle's disappointment than his own. 'We'll soon have that stuff out of the way.'

Dickpa was examining a pile of loose boulders that lay at the foot of the cliff and spread far into the stream, so far indeed that its course had been slightly altered.

'Well, let's get at it,' went on Biggles, throwing down his bundle. 'It isn't such a bad spot; we've plenty of water, anyway.'

The stores were heaped on the bank and all four of them were soon hard at work prising and dragging down the rocks that concealed the entrance of the cave.

'This isn't the only place where the rock has fallen, by the look of it,' said Dickpa once, during a brief rest, pointing farther along the base of the cliff where several piles of rock, similar to the one on which they were working, lay strewn about. 'I fancy there must have been a bit of an earthquake, since I was here last, to bring all this stuff down.'

'Well, as long as there isn't another, to bring another lot down on our heads while we're here, I don't mind,' observed Biggles, resuming his task. 'Do they get many earthquakes here?'

'I don't think anybody's been here long enough to see,' replied Dickpa with a smile, 'but I don't think so; at least, not in recent years. The whole country is volcanic, of course, and once upon a time it must have been pretty bad. It was an earthquake that split these mountains about like that,' he went on, pointing at several wide fissures higher up in the face of the cliff. 'There's not much more to shift, thank goodness; we're lucky it's no worse,' he concluded.

But appearances were deceptive, and with only their hands, a small crowbar, a hammer, and a chisel, that had been brought to break down the wall inside, to work with, it was well into the afternoon before the Inca rock carving was exposed to full view.

'You see the luck of it,' said Dickpa during another pause. 'For hundreds of years this place has stood just as it was when the Incas left it. Then I happened to come along—perhaps the first man since they went away—and I spotted that tell-tale mark. Then, before the year is out, down comes all this rock and hides the whole thing up. But for the fact that I had already seen the carving and the cave, and knew they were here, what chance would there have been of anyone ever finding them under all this stuff? It would probably have remained undiscovered until eternity. Well, one thing is certain; we shan't have time to break down the wall today. We dare not risk being benighted so far away from the machine,' he continued, glancing up at the now sinking sun. 'Naturally I didn't expect this or

91

we might have brought the hammocks and enough food to last us a day or two. But that's Brazil all over; the unexpected is always happening—'

'Hark!' The exclamation came from Biggles, on whose face appeared a look of utter incredulous amazement.

Faint but clear from the far distance came the unmistakable hum of a powerful aero engine. They all stared in the direction from which the sound came in stupefied astonishment, and for some time nobody spoke.

'I'm not dreaming, Algy, am I?' asked Biggles anxiously. 'Can you hear it too?'

'There's no question about it,' replied Algy promptly. 'It's the machine all right.'

'But who on earth could have found it, and, what is more miraculous, who in these parts could fly it even if they found it?' cried Biggles angrily. 'It isn't sense.'

'Sense or not,' snapped Algy, 'I can see it—there she is. Look!' He pointed with a trembling finger.

'They must have followed us up the river,' muttered Dickpa through set teeth, 'and they've brought a pilot with them.'

'No!' yelled Biggles, who had been staring fixedly at the distant speck in the sky. 'That isn't the *Condor*; it's a twin engine job. It's too far off to say for certain, but it looks to me like one of those American Curtiss flying-boats.'

'So that's why they went to New Orleans,' said Dickpa quickly, with a flash of understanding. 'The devils! They saw us fly away and guessed what we were going to do. If they made enquiries they'd find we had bought a machine. They cut across to New Orleans and got another—with a pilot, too, for none of them could fly. This is going to complicate matters.'

'Complicate!' cried Biggles. 'It's going to do more

than that, if I'm any judge. They're not coming this way, thank goodness. They're looking for us, no doubt, but they are going back down the river now, I think. We'd better get back ourselves, and quickly, too.'

Dickpa took a swift look around the work they had done. 'Yes, I think so,' he replied. 'We've only a few more minutes' work here and we shall have a hole large enough to enable us to get in. It's really better that it should be left as it is until we have coped with this new development.'

'All right, let's get away then,' returned Biggles. 'I shan't feel happy until I feel the *Condor* under my feet again. We shall have to hide her from aerial observation in future, although that shouldn't be difficult in a place like this. As soon as we have done that, we can come back here and go on working quietly. They won't be likely to see us; we shall be more likely to see them.'

'It seems a pity,' said Dickpa, looking reflectively at the top of the cave, which they could now see. 'So near and yet so far. Well, it can't be helped. We might as well leave the tools here; there is no need to carry them backwards and forwards.'

A cache was quickly made of the equipment they had brought with them and they set out on their journey back to the machine. Biggles climbed up on the bank of the stream and surveyed the rolling prairie abstractedly.

'What are you looking at?' asked Algy casually.

'Oh, I was just wondering,' answered Biggles.

'Wondering what?'

'As a matter of fact, I was wondering if it was possible to put the machine down here,' replied Biggles, removing a bee from his ear. 'This new development is a bit of a boneshaker. Who would have thought

93

they'd do such a thing? I wonder what sort of pilot they've got.'

'They'd have no difficulty in getting a pilot with the machine, particularly if the prospect of treasure was mentioned,' declared Dickpa, leading the way through the shallows on the edge of the stream. 'But come on, we shall have to put our best foot forward or we shall be caught in the dark. It's no joke groping your way through the forest after dark, I can assure you. I've had some of it.'

With their own trail to follow back and unencumbered with the tools, they reached the edge of the forest belt in good time, and, following the path they had cut in the morning through the forest, were able to keep up a steady pace.

'I shan't be sorry to get back,' admitted Algy, mopping the perspiration from his face. 'Gosh, isn't it hot? But for these confounded flies this would be a really nice place to spend a holiday. Think what a collection of butterflies you could make,' he went on, pointing to a cloud of huge brilliant-coloured butterflies that rose from the path in front of him.

'Well, here we are—' began Biggles as they emerged into the clearing, but he stopped dead, staring. The others lined up beside him and stood silent; there was no need for words. The *Condor* had gone.

Dickpa was the first to recover from the shock of this staggering discovery. He darted forward and peered up and down the river. 'Not a sign of it,' he snapped, and then turned to examine the ground on the edge of the water. He stooped, picked up the butt end of a cigar, and then pitched it carelessly into the water with an expressive shrug of his shoulders. 'That tells us all we need to know,' he said quietly. 'I blame myself—'

'Blame nobody,' interrupted Biggles crisply. 'No one

on earth could have anticipated this. Who would think of camouflaging a machine in such a place? Pah, don't be silly, Dickpa. There's a limit to the foresight one might be expected to have, and this is outside it, by a long way. We might have guessed they would see the *Condor* when we were over there at the cave, but, quite frankly, the thought never occurred to me. The only possible danger that crossed my mind was the Indians, but it seemed so unlikely that the *Condor* could be seen from the main stream that I had no fears about leaving her here. Even if we had known what they were up to, it would have made no difference; we couldn't have got back in time to do anything. It's no use talking about blame or what might have been.'

'That's right,' agreed Dickpa; 'let's face the facts. What they amount to is this: we're stranded high and dry, without food and without a boat, in what is just about the hardest place in the world to get out of. The position is serious, very serious, and it's no use pretending it isn't, but we're not dead yet—'

'Not by a long chalk,' broke in Biggles savagely. 'There's only one thing to do, so we might as well set about it. We've got to get the machine back.'

'An admirable plan, but one which seems to present a little difficulty,' observed Dickpa, a trifle sarcastically. 'By working really hard we might make two or three miles a day along the river bank. You can work it out yourself how long it will take us to get five hundred miles. I don't want to appear pessimistic, but, as you say, we must face the facts.'

'I'm not doing any walking back,' replied Biggles shortly. 'You don't suppose I was thinking of walking back to Manaos, to be chucked into prison when I got there?' he went on grimly. 'We've got to see about getting a boat.'

'All right. We'd better start making one. I—'

'Hold hard, let me finish,' interrupted Biggles. 'I've just remembered something, and it might be a trump card. I believe we can get the *Condor* back, but let's take one thing at a time. The first thing we've got to have is a canoe. Well, there happens to be one lying on the beach on the opposite bank, a mile or two higher up. I'll tell you later how I know it's there. Wait here while I go and fetch it.'

'You're not thinking of trying to swim the river, are you?'

'As I can neither fly nor walk on water without sinking, I can't think of any alternative,' replied Biggles, stripping off his jacket.

'But you're crazy, man. You wouldn't get half way without being pulled down by crocs. This is where I come in,' declared Dickpa. 'Let's start and knock up a *balsa*.'

'A what?'

'*Balsa*—a raft made of reeds. They use them a lot in Bolivia—in fact, they make their boats that way. It will only be rough, but it might float long enough to see you across to the other side. It's worth trying, anyway. I remember seeing plenty of reeds a little higher up. Algy, you bend a bamboo into a hoop and cover it with a piece of your shirt, or anything you like, to make a paddle. Come on, Smyth, and you, Biggles,' concluded Dickpa, leading the way into the bushes.

In five minutes they were hard at work cutting down the reeds, tying them into bundles, and binding them tightly with lianas, of which there were plenty to hand and which made quite passable substitutes for ropes. The bundles were lashed together side by side and then another layer fastened on top. It was quite dark by the time the job was done and the improvised raft dragged down into the water. It floated—sluggishly it is true, and settled fairly deep in the water when Biggles crawled cautiously on to it. 'Give me that paddle, Algy,' he said quickly; 'she won't float long.'

Algy passed the primitive paddle, and Biggles pushed the frail craft away from the bank with a quick shove. 'I shan't be long,' came his voice from the darkness. 'Wait where you are, and, if you hear me whistle, answer. Cheerio.'

Once in the river proper, Biggles paddled furiously for the opposite bank about two hundred yards away. Half way across he could feel that the flimsy raft had settled a lot deeper in the water, and progress became slower. It was difficult to keep straight, and for every few yards of headway he made he drifted farther downstream with the current. He was still fifty yards from the bank when it became completely submerged, but it still supported him, and he flung his weight behind the paddle.

A long, sinister shadow broke the surface of the water close behind him, a shadow that cut a fine ripple in the still water and began to overtake him. Biggles knew quite well what it was; a crocodile had scented him and was hard on his trail. The water was half way up his body now, and, realising that the raft no longer afforded any protection against the impending attack of the monster, and that he could in fact travel faster by swimming, he flung the paddle aside and struck out in a swift overarm stroke for the shore. It was a racing stroke, and one that he could not keep up for long, but he had only a short distance to cover, and he flung himself ashore in a last frantic spurt. Even as he did so, something like an iron gate clashed just behind his heels.

He darted across the beach and then paused for

breath, trembling slightly, for the strain of the last two moments had been intense. Opportunely, the crescent moon rose above the treetops and shed a silvery radiance over the scene. He watched a long, log-like object slowly submerging in the water near the bank, and then, with a shudder, turned his face resolutely towards the hut and its grisly tenant. It was nervy work, this picking his way among the fantastic shadows on the shore of an uncharted river, more trying even than flying through a sky swarming with enemy aircraft. They at least were tangible, real, and something he understood, but here he was faced with unknown dangers and factors outside his experience. The black, impenetrable forest wall was a curtain that concealed— what? He did not know, but furtive rustlings helped his imagination to visualize horrors that crawled and slithered through the ooze. Every shadow was a menace that might hold some denizen of the forest or the black oily river waiting and watching for its prey.

Once he stopped while a monstrous crab with tall, stilt-like legs and waving antennæ marched with a curious clicking noise across the beach into the water, and a few moments later, passing across the shadows of some tangled ropelike lianas, one of them came to life and glided, as silent as the shadows themselves, into the forest. For a second Biggles came near to panicking, but he set his teeth and hurried on, brushing away with his shirt-sleeve the beads of icy perspiration that gathered on his forehead.

The hut came into view at last, and he hesitated, striking irritably at a great white moth that hovered over his head. Somehow the flimsy walls looked very different in the pale light of the moon from what they had done in the bright light of day, but he knew it was the memory of what they concealed that prompted his misgivings. 'Bah! Dead men don't bite,' he muttered harshly, and, wondering vaguely where he had heard or read the words, he strode swiftly towards the canoe. He was bending over it, clearing the debris from the bottom, when a sound reached his ears that sent the blood draining from his face and seemed to freeze his heart into a ball of ice. Something had moved inside the hut.

He did not stir a finger, but turned his eyes towards it, staring. They confirmed what his eyes had told him; the roof of the hut was swaying—only slightly, but moving beyond all shadow of doubt. He ceased to breathe, listening. Silence. The scene, which was engraved on Biggles's memory for ever, was wrapped in a silence so complete and utter that it seemed to press on him. A wave of unreality swept over him; that it was not true, that he was dreaming, a horrid nightmare from which he would presently awake. He felt that he was a detached spectator, something apart, watching, as it were, a silent film. How long he remained thus he did not know, for time had ceased to be. It might have been a minute, five minutes, or even ten; he was never able to say; but he was just beginning to breathe again when the silence was broken by a low choking moan that ended in something like a drawn-out sob.

For the first time in his life Biggles knew the meaning of the word fear—stark, paralysing fear. He tried to move, to run, to place himself as far as possible from the accursed place, but his limbs refused to function. His mouth had turned bone dry, so dry that his tongue clove to it. He could only stare. Then, with a crash that broke the spell, the loose reeds parted, and a dark form leapt to the ground. At the same instant Biggles sprang to his feet. Before him, not ten yards away, stood a black panther, its eyes gleaming and its tail swishing to and fro like that of an angry cat. For perhaps a second, man and beast faced each other, and then, before the man could move, the beast bounded lightly away into the forest and disappeared.

In his relief Biggles laughed aloud, a sound so horrible that he broke off in the middle realizing with a shock that he was near hysteria. 'This won't do,' he snarled, furious with himself for so nearly breaking down, for the whole thing was plain enough now. The beast's presence in the hut was natural enough, and he had no doubt as to the ghastly object of its visit. 'I shall feel better when I turn my back on this place,' he muttered as he turned to the canoe.

It was in rather worse condition than he had expected. As usual with canoes used in such places, it had been cut out of a solid tree and was about twenty feet long. It was rotten in many places, as he quickly discovered when he tried to move it, for a piece of the freeboard came away in his hand, leaving an ugly gap. It was heavy, and he was afraid of using all his strength to move it in case it collapsed altogether. He hunted around and soon found two bamboo poles. Using these as rollers, he slipped the canoe smoothly across the narrow strip of beach, and floated on the placid surface of the river.

There was only one paddle, but fortunately it was of hard wood and still in fairly good condition, so, taking his seat in the stern, he drove the canoe towards the opposite bank. He found that the primitive craft had not been cut quite true and, at first, steering was rather awkward, but he soon became accustomed to its peculiarities and was able to keep a fairly straight and speedy course towards the backwater where the others awaited him. He experienced no difficulty in finding them, for they were evidently keeping a sharp look-out and his low whistle was immediately answered from the darkness.

'Good work,' exclaimed Dickpa enthusiastically as the nose of the canoe grounded. 'You were gone rather a long time, though, and gave us a rare fright.'

'Nothing to the fright I gave myself,' Biggles assured him, pleased with the success of his mission.

'What happened?'

'I'll tell you about it some other time,' answered Biggles. 'If I talk about it now I shall have the heebie-jeebies. We've no time to lose, anyway. I've been thinking of our best plan as I paddled across, and this, I think, is it. If you can think of a better one, say so.'

'Go ahead,' invited Dickpa.

'Righto. Now, Silas & Co. are somewhere downstream—'

'Are you sure of that?'

'Pretty well sure. There were several nice landing-places below us—we passed them on the way up—but there are only one or two rather risky places above us. They came up the river looking for us, and spotted the machine right away, as they were almost certain to. They landed and found no one at home. Fine. What did they do? They simply took the *Condor* in tow and pushed off to a place which would suit them as a base while they were looking for us. Now we've two things in our favour. In the first place, they will probably think we shall be away two or three days at least, and secondly, they'll fancy themselves quite safe if they moor up on the opposite side of the river, because they will not imagine for a moment that we have any means of getting across. That's where they've boobed. They won't be expecting us, and may not even keep a watch. Right! Our first business is to locate them, and that's got to be done before morning, before they set out to locate *us*. Having found them, we split up, one party to make a feint attack from the shore while the others cut out the machine. Algy and I will have to go for the machine; that's automatic, because we're pilots, and if one of us gets hurt the other can carry on.

'You, Dickpa, and Smyth, make up the shore party. When we've spotted the machine, we'll pull into the bank and let you land. Algy and I will cross over to the other side, creep along the bank, and try to slip across without being spotted. We'll synchronize our watches, and at a certain time, which we'll fix, Algy and I will board the *Condor* and cut her loose. If we can do that and drift away without being discovered, well and good, but if we're spotted you will open fire from a position commanding their camp, which you will have already taken up. Get that clear, because in a show of this sort, perfect timing and absolute adherence to plan is necessary. Zero hour will depend on what time we find them, provided, of course, we do find them. We can make twelve or fourteen miles before dawn, although they should not be all that far away. At the time we fix, Algy and I will board the *Condor*. If an alarm is given, you must kick up the biggest row you can. In the confusion we shall cut and run for it. Speed will be everything. If the engine starts easily, we might even get away before they grasp what is going on, and if you keep up a fairly rapid fire, that will keep them under cover. We may get a chance to damage their machine, but I shan't take any risks to do it; our job is to get our own. If we succeed in doing that, they won't see us for dust and small pebbles. Well, how does that sound to you?'

'I don't think I can better it,' admitted Dickpa. 'Surprise is the most valuable asset in any attack, and we have that in our favour. Assuming that you get the *Condor*, what is the next move? What about Smyth and I?'

'We shall taxi the *Condor* up the river, and assuming that all goes well, pick you up where we put you ashore. You may be pursued—or so may we, if it comes to that—but we shall have to leave that to chance. We shall keep a look-out for you on the bank; I don't think we can fix anything more definite than that. What do you think about it, Algy? Can you think of anything we've overlooked, or you, Smyth?'

'What about weapons?' asked Algy.

'What have we got? The 12-bore and the Express. Dickpa and Smyth will have to take those, of course. We shan't need any—or at least I don't think so. If the thing ends in a pitched battle at close range, the machine will be knocked about for a certainty, and we must avoid that at all costs. I expect we shall come in for a warm time if they spot us, and if they do we shall simply have to bolt for it. Anything else?'

The final question was greeted with silence, so Biggles turned in the direction of the canoe. 'All aboard, then,' he said. Without further ado they took their places in the dead man's dugout. It carried them comfortably, for, although its crew had normally consisted of one member, it was designed to carry a fairly large cargo of rubber, which weighs heavily. So the canoe, while low in the water, accommodated them well. Biggles, with the Express across his knees, took the look-out post in front, whilst Dickpa, on account of his long experience in the handling of such craft, took the paddle. The others sat between them, Algy watching the left bank and Smyth the right. Like a shadow they slipped out of the backwater, and, keeping in the heavy shade near the bank, were soon gliding swiftly downstream.

An hour passed slowly. No one spoke; the steady swish of the paddle was the only sound that marked their progress. Each bend, as they approached it, was taken slowly and cautiously, Biggles straining his eyes forward into the gloom for signs of their enemies. A quarter of an hour later he uttered a warning, 'Hist!' and raised his hand above his head. Dickpa twisted the paddle deep in the water and pulled the canoe up in its own length, edging in towards the shore.

'Easy all,' breathed Biggles. 'There they are.'

'About half a mile away, I should judge,' observed Dickpa quietly, with his eyes fixed on a fire on the opposite bank. It was only a small camp fire, but against the pitch black silhouette of the forest it showed up like a beacon.

'What's the time by your watch, Dickpa?' asked Biggles.

'Twelve thirty-four.'

'Good. I'll set mine the same. How will one-thirty a.m. suit for zero hour? That should give you ample time to reach them. You may have time to spare, but that's better than underdoing it. I suppose you can find your way through the forest?'

'I never move without my compass,' replied Dickpa shortly. 'One-thirty is the time, then.'

'Righto! We all know what we have to do. Straight across to the other bank, Dickpa.'

Five minutes later the canoe scraped her nose on the sandy bank of a bend, which afforded a good landing-place out of sight of the enemy camp.*

* Many South American rivers have sand or mud beaches on alternate sides where the rivers bend, due to silt being brought down in time of floods.

An almost inaudible 'Cheerio—good luck!' came from the bank, and then Dickpa and Smyth were swallowed up in the Stygian darkness of the forest belt. For some minutes Biggles and Algy were silent.

'No hurry,' said Biggles at last. 'We must give them a good start. They're bound to be a lot longer getting there than we shall. It's better to hang about here than lower down, where we might be seen. My word, isn't it hot?'

'I don't mind the heat so much; it's the mosquitoes that get me down,' groaned Algy. 'They're tearing me to pieces.'

Again silence fell. Occasionally a noise reached them from farther down the river of firewood being cut, or the rattle of a tin can or plate. The waiting, as is always the case, was a weary and nerve-trying period, and Algy was thankful when Biggles at last announced that it was time they were moving.

They backed the canoe high enough up the river to ensure that it could not be seen from the enemy camp as they crossed over to the opposite bank, and then began stealthily edging along in the deepest shadows. They were soon in line with the now smouldering embers of the camp fire, and they pointed the nose of the canoe towards it. They were half way over before the dim outlines of two aeroplanes became dimly visible, and Biggles rested on his paddle to study the position of the enemy camp. The fire had been built on a flat, sandy beach, and around it were four recumbent human forms. A fifth, who had evidently been left on guard, was sitting upright with a gun across his knees; as they watched, he added a handful of fuel to the fire, which caused it to burn up brightly and cast a ruddy glow over the scene, across which danced fantastic flickering shadows. Near the group was a pile of stores, and a little farther away a good-sized stack of familiar, square petrol-tins.

About ten yards from the shore a twin-engined flying-boat was moored, the one they had seen in the air and which could now be identified as a Curtiss, the type Biggles had named. Near it, so close that their wing-tips almost touched, was the *Condor*. The sentry was obviously not keeping a very good look-out, which did not surprise them, for the enemy had little reason to suppose that they had anything to fear from the stranded treasure-seekers. Nevertheless, the pilots realized that in the dead silence of the tropic night the slightest sound could not fail to be heard.

Biggles glanced at his wristwatch. 'Ten minutes to go,' he breathed in Algy's ear, manœuvring the canoe so that the aeroplanes came between the sentry's line of vision and themselves. Very slowly, and with hardly a ripple, they crept nearer, until at last the canoe gently touched the side of the *Condor*. Algy, who had already removed his boots and hung them round his neck by the laces, crept aboard and lay behind the big metal propeller in readiness for action. Biggles looked again at his watch; the time was one twenty-nine, one minute to zero hour. With infinite patience he began edging the canoe towards the nose of the amphibian, and, reaching it, he quietly sawed through the rope by which it was moored. Then, still keeping on the off side from the sentry, he crept like a wraith into the cockpit. A fleeting glance showed the abandoned canoe, clear of the hull, drifting slowly down the stream.

For perhaps a couple of minutes Biggles thought they were going to float away unobserved without a shot being fired, but in this he was doomed to disappointment. Just as they were almost clear of the Curtiss a stray slant of wind swung them round slightly, so that their wing-tip touched the elevators of the other machine. The noise made was negligible, merely a scraping jar that ended in a soft splash as the other machine righted itself, but it was sufficient to bring the sentry to his feet. For an instant he stared at the amphibian, now moving perceptibly as it felt the current, and then he let out a wild yell. He flung up his gun, and its report blended with two others that roared out from the pitch black forest wall. Simultaneously pandemonium broke loose. Biggles snapped, 'Swing her, Algy,' as he turned on the petrol, lost in a babble of sound from the bank, which, from a picture of peace, had become a howling bedlam. Above a shrill medley of sounds punctuated with the crashing reports of guns and the clanging of metal as some bullets struck the stack of petrol-tins, Biggles heard Algy's sharp, 'Contact!' He whirled the self-starter, and the engine came to life with a bellow of sound that added to the frightful uproar.

The men on the bank, awakened from a deep sleep, and clearly at a loss to know exactly what was happening except that they were obviously being attacked from the land, now turned their attention to this new development. A volley of shots rang out, and one or two bullets ripped through the fabric of the *Condor*.

But Biggles was taxi-ing now, swinging round in a wide circle to face upstream. Rat-tat-tat-tat-tat-tat-tat-tat—he caught himself flinching as a machine-gun started its erratic stutter, spraying the amphibian and the surrounding water with a shower of lead. He opened the throttle a little wider, racing as fast as he dared without actually leaving the water, to escape the leaden hail. With his eyes fixed intently ahead, he caught his breath as they fell upon a big, black object lying right across their path. A broken, jagged arm flung itself upwards, and he knew it was a great tree turning slowly over and over as it floated towards the sea. He knew that to strike such an obstacle at the rate they were travelling would tear the keel out of the amphibian as if it were so much tissue paper. Stop, he could not, neither was there time to turn to avoid it. Automatically, he took the only course open to him; he thrust the throttle wide open and, as the machine leapt forward, jerked the joystick back into his stomach. The threshing smother of foam dropped away below and astern as the *Condor* soared upwards like a bird into the starry tropic sky.

At a thousand feet Biggles flattened out and looked about him. Below lay the river, gleaming in the silvery radiance of the moon. On both sides, stretching away into the infinite distance, was the forest, black and forbidding. Below he could see the camp with the fire shining like a red star that had fallen upon the beach. He glanced around at the low door that communicated with the cabin, wondering why Algy did not join him, at the same time heading for their old landing-place higher up the river. He was anxious to put the machine down as quickly as possible, not because there was any particular danger in staying aloft, but because he wished to pick up Dickpa and Smyth, and in any case they could not afford to go on using petrol. Their only real danger lay in the landing, which, without flares, would have been difficult enough at night in a land place, but in the present circumstances called for much greater skill and judgement. Turning his head farther round, he made out the silhouette of Algy leaning out of the rear cockpit; he seemed to be trying to attract his attention, waving his arms and pointing.

Then he saw something else, something that at first brought a puzzled frown to his face, an expression that quickly turned to one of horror when he made out what it was. On top of the hull, just in front of the engine, was a large, black pile, like a thick coiled rope. The end seemed to be waving in the air, lashing to and fro in the rush of the wind. Then it began to uncoil and writhe towards him. Algy disappeared from the cockpit.

For a moment Biggles's war-acquired calm almost deserted him; his mind seemed to work sluggishly at this final overwhelming horror. That it was a snake he knew, and a big one at that—a huge water-snake that had, in the quiet of the night, crawled up onto the warm, dry hull. And now, disliking the noise and rush of wind, it was moving about, looking for a way to escape and prepared to attack the disturbers of its peace.

Biggles hardly knew what to do for the best. Instinctively he had started side-slipping down towards the river, his one paramount thought being to get on the ground at any cost before the horror caught him in its coils, and by dragging him from the joystick hurl them both to oblivion in the black void below. Whatever happened, he knew he could not let go of the joystick; if he had to fight it would be with one arm only, and with such a handicap the fight could only end one way. He started as Algy, his lips parted and a look of utter horror in his eyes, crept through the cabin door and stood up beside him; in his hand he held one of the heavy knives they had brought for cutting their way through the forest. He saw him raise the weapon and strike at something behind him. The machine lurched sickeningly, and he turned his attention to keeping it on an even keel above the river. He could see their old landing-place about two miles ahead, but immediately below them the river twisted and turned in a manner that made a landing out of the question. To collide with the wall of the forest at the speed they were travelling would be as fatal as anything the snake could do.

Suddenly he realized that Algy had disappeared, but, turning farther, he saw a sight that seemed to freeze the blood in his veins. Algy, with a thick coil wound about his body, was hanging on with one hand to a centre-section bracing strut; with the other he was hacking furiously at a broad black shadow that lashed about like a wind-stocking in a gale.

But they were near the water now. Hardly knowing what he was doing, Biggles throttled back and flattened out over the lagoon. Could Algy hold out until they were on the water was the thought that raced over and over again, like an endless chain through his head. Just as the keel swished lightly on the surface there was a sudden lurch and two or three loud splashes, as if things were dropping from the machine. Without waiting for the *Condor* to finish her run, he let go of the joystick, and, turning, sprang to his feet. Algy and the snake had disappeared. He dropped back into his seat with a jerk, and with stick and rudder hard over, flung the machine round into its own wake. 'Br-r-r-r-r! Brrr-r-r-r-r! Brrrr-r-r-r-r-r!' roared the engine spasmodically as he opened the throttle in short, quick jerks. 'Algy!' he yelled hysterically. 'Algy!'

'Here,' came a feeble voice not far away.

Biggles taxied swiftly to the spot and saw Algy's white face in the water. It was the work of a moment to reach over and drag him neck and crop into the cockpit, where he collapsed limply on to the seat.

'Are you alright, kid?' asked Biggles anxiously.

Algy passed his hand wearily over his face. 'Yes, I'm alright,' he said slowly. 'Strewth, what a night we're having! I thought it was all up that time.'

110

'So did I,' agreed Biggles. 'What happened to the snake?'

'The bits of it went overboard.'

'Bits of it?'

'Yes, I think it must have been a python, or a boa constrictor, because I've read they have to get a purchase round something with their tail when they start the squeezing business. That fellow had me pinned to the strut and then tried to get his tail round something.'

'Well?'

'First of all he tried the engine, but it was a bit too hot for him. I heard him sizzle, and he sprang back like a bit of elastic. Then he tried the prop, but that was worse; it went through him like a knife going through a sausage and he literally went to bits, in every sense of the word. A lump hit me across the back of the neck and knocked me overboard. But where are Dickpa and Smyth?'

'My word, yes, we shall have to go back for them. The show went off all right, but, as usual, the unforeseen happened. I didn't reckon on tree-trunks and snakes.'

'Tree-trunk, was it? I couldn't think what you were up to when we shot into the air. I thought you'd gone balmy.'

'I nearly did, and so would you. We seem to have had a merry evening, one way and another.'

'But what had we better do about the others?'

'There's only one thing we can do—taxi slowly down the bank looking for them. What's the matter?'

Algy, who was sniffing the air, looking around slowly. 'Can you smell petrol?' he asked anxiously.

Biggles started. 'I can,' he said briefly. 'There's a leak somewhere. Confound it! That's going to be awkward.'

A few minutes' search disclosed the trouble; a bullet had passed clean through the main tank. Frantically they began plugging the hole, but presently gave it up, realising it was too late to do any good; the precious liquid had gone beyond recovery, leaving the tank dry.

'That's just about torn it,' observed Biggles calmly. 'I've been flying on the special tank, so there can't be much left in it. There may be enough for half an hour's flying in the gravity tank* and there is a little in the tins in the cabin. It's better than nothing, but it isn't enough—not half enough—to get us back.'

Algy did not speak.

'Never mind, it can't be helped,' went on Biggles. 'Let's settle one thing at a time. Before we do anything else we must find Dickpa and Smyth. We'll settle what we're going to do afterwards.'

They turned the machine and taxied quickly, but carefully down the river, above which they had just had such a hideous experience. Presently Biggles throttled back and cruised more slowly, while Algy watched the bank closely.

'There they are!' he called suddenly.

The *Condor* swung round almost in its own length and nosed in towards the bank, where two figures were gesticulating frantically. They ceased when they saw the machine standing in towards them, and a minute later Dickpa and Smyth clambered over the side. Without waiting for explanations, Biggles turned again and taxied upstream as quickly as he dared to their original landing-place, taking care to moor on the opposite bank to the one where the Indians had made their unexpected attack.

---

* A back-up tank of petrol which feeds petrol into the engine without the use of a petrol pump, using gravity instead.

'Well, here we are,' announced Biggles. 'Are you all right, Dickpa—and you, Smyth?'

'Right as rain,' came the reply. 'We had no trouble at all. You seem to have had all the fun.'

'Fun!' cried Biggles incredulously. 'Fun you call it! If you call aviating in the middle of the night across an unknown forest, with a mad snake for a passenger, fun, you've got a queer sense of humour.'

Briefly he related the story of their enforced flight and its nearly tragic ending. 'I don't know about you,' he concluded, 'but before I can do anything else I must have some sleep. I'm about all in. Smyth, you'd better see about repairing the hole in the tank at the crack of dawn.'

Smyth nodded.

'We'd better sleep on board as best we can,' observed Dickpa, 'and we shall have to take turns to keep watch. We can't afford to take any more chances with those gentry down the river.'

Chapter 10
The Raid

Biggles was awakened at the first streak of dawn by Smyth working on the damaged tank. He felt a different man after the rest, and assisted the mechanic in his work, which was finished to their satisfaction by the time the others were moving. It was not a very clean job, but as good as could be expected in the circumstances, and with the help of that well-known stand-by of long distance airmen, chewing-gum, which Biggles had brought for the purpose, the hole was plugged sufficiently well to hold petrol until such time as a more permanent repair could be effected. The spare petrol was brought from the cabin and poured into the tank and the empty tins sunk in the river.

'What's the next move?' asked Dickpa crisply, as they made a substantial breakfast of bacon and biscuits from their stores.

'To get out of the way as soon as we can,' replied Biggles. 'They'll come up the river looking for us as soon as it's light enough, and as they have a machine-gun they are likely to make things awkward. We can't hide on the river—they're bound to find us—which means that we've got to find somewhere else. The thing that worries me is this shortage of petrol.'

'I've never heard of anything so absurd as this in my life,' snorted Dickpa. 'Could you imagine anything more utterly impossible than two aeroplanes chasing each other up and down an unknown river in the heart of South America?'

'I can do more than imagine,' grunted Biggles, making for the cockpit. 'I can hear 'em—or at least one of 'em. Hark!'

Far away, the unmistakable sound of an aero engine could be heard, gradually drawing nearer. Biggles listened intently, with his head on one side, for a moment. 'That machine isn't in the air; it's running on about quarter throttle. They're taxi-ing up the river to make sure of finding us. What do you say, Smyth?'

'They're taxi-ing all right,' agreed the mechanic instantly, to whom the sound of an aero engine was familiar music.

'And that's where they're making a mistake,' returned Biggles at once. 'They won't hear us for the noise of their own engine. By Jove—'

'Well, what is it?' enquired Algy.

'I was wondering if it might not be a good moment to solve this petrol problem.'

'How?'

'They've got plenty on the beach. They will all be on the machine, or most of them will. By Jingo, it's worth trying!'

'But how—'

'I'll show you,' replied Biggles promptly, 'but we've no time to lose. Swing the prop, Smyth.'

The others took their places while the mechanic turned the propeller to suck petrol gas into the cylinders. 'Contact!' he called, and stepped down into the cabin.

The engine started easily, and Biggles throttled back until it was ticking over musically to allow it to warm up. Then he taxied out to the middle of the stream and, after a careful survey for floating trees or other obstructions, opened the throttle. The *Condor* raced across the water and then soared into the air.

For a full ten minutes Biggles followed a course still farther up the river than they had yet been, climbing steadily all the time. Then, judging that he had gone far enough and had acquired sufficient altitude to pass unobserved, he swung round in a wide curve and flew back in the direction of the enemy camp, keeping parallel with, but at some distance from, the river. Algy, who now perceived Biggles's plan, judged that they were a good ten miles from the river, so it would be almost impossible for the crew of the searching flying-boat to see them. For nearly half an hour Biggles flew thus, and then he turned once more towards the river. Reaching it, he again flew upstream, approaching the enemy camp from the opposite direction. They were now some miles below the Curtiss, but travelling in the same direction.

He followed the river for a few minutes and then, finding a stretch long enough for a comfortable landing, dropped down on the smooth surface of the water.

'What I've done,' he explained to the others, 'is to fly round roughly in a circle. I flew straight on at first until I was sure we were out of both sight and earshot, and then came right round in a circle to strike the river below the enemy camp. The position now is this. The Curtiss is just about at the place where we spent the night—perhaps they have already passed it. Knowing—or rather imagining—that we're still in front of them somewhere, as we went off in that direction last night, they'll keep going on, thinking that sooner or later they are bound to come up with us. That's where they're wrong, of course. We are now about five or six miles below the camp where we surprised them last night. I am hoping that the petrol is still on the bank, because there seems to be no object in their dragging it about with them.

'Now what I suggest is this,' he went on. 'There is just a chance that they have left no one in charge of the camp; if they have, it won't be more than one man, or two at the most. When we have taxied as near as we dare without risking being heard, three of us will go ashore and raid the camp. If anyone is there, we'll hold them up at gun point. Having done that, whoever is left in charge of the *Condor* will taxi up and get the petrol on board. Then we'll hop it.'

'Where to?' asked Algy in surprise.

'One thing at a time,' replied Biggles impatiently. 'Let's get the juice first. I shall feel a lot happier with the tanks full.'

Without further delay they started taxi-ing up the river, throttling back the engine as far as they could to make as little noise as possible. When they had approached as near as they dared, they edged up to the bank.

'I'm going with the shore party this time,' declared Algy.

Biggles was inclined to argue, but Dickpa cut him short. 'You're captain of the ship,' he declared, 'so it is only right that you should stay with it. If you hear three shots in quick succession at regular intervals, you'll know we've captured the camp; then all you have to do is to taxi up as fast as you can.'

Biggles nodded. 'Good enough,' he agreed. 'Go ahead.'

Dickpa, closely followed by Algy and Smyth, all suitably armed, stepped into the shallow water beside the bow and waded ashore.

'Keep close behind me and don't make more noise than you can help,' said Dickpa quietly. 'We're bound to make a bit of a row, because we shall have to cut our path in places. You do the cutting, Smyth, while I carry the compass.'

The next hour was to live in Algy's mind for a long while; the heat was appalling and the insects dreadful. Bees crawled all over them, while stings and bites from the other pests that settled on them, or crawled up their legs from the ground, uncomfortably demonstrated that Dickpa's description of the discomforts of travelling in Brazil was, if anything, understated. To touch an overhanging branch, either by accident or design, was to dislodge an army of ants that attacked them viciously. They affected Dickpa least, because, as he pointed out, he was more or less accustomed to them — not that this made the stings less venomous. After what seemed an eternity they saw the river ahead through the trees and long trailing lianas. There was no beach at that particular point, however, so they continued through the forest, keeping parallel with the water.

A silent signal from Dickpa warned them that they were near their destination and there could be no more hacking at the undergrowth that blocked their path. Each liana had to be severed separately and quietly, and progress was consequently slow. They came upon the beach quite suddenly. Dickpa gently parted the green curtain in front of them and there it was, the stores and equipment lying about and the pile of petrol-tins just as they had last seen them. A man was sitting on a pile of blankets, smoking and staring upstream as if watching for the return of the flying-boat; he was about forty yards away. They scanned the beach from end to end for others of the party, but could see none, so with their guns at the ready they advanced over the soft sand towards the unsuspecting man.

He must have been dozing, for he did not move until they were right on him, and only then when Dickpa

118

spoke. The words were in Portuguese, so the others did not understand what he said, except the word 'Philippe,' and Algy stared at Dickpa's old carrier, who had really been the whole cause of the trouble. The man now presented a pitiable spectacle. Dickpa had described him as a coward, and this his actions quickly proved him to be. He burst into tears and flung himself at his late master's feet, obviously begging him to spare his life.

Dickpa spurned him away with his foot. 'The cowardly villain,' he said. 'He thinks we shall do what he himself would do if the positions were reversed—cut his throat. Keep your gun on him, Smyth, and don't take your eyes off him for an instant, for he is as treacherous as he is cowardly. We can't kill him in cold blood, although goodness knows he deserves it, but if he tries any monkey-tricks—shoot.'

Dickpa pointed his rifle into the sky and pulled the trigger three times quickly, at regular intervals; the distant roar of the *Condor*'s engine told them at once that the pilot had heard the signal. Presently they saw him swing round the bend and race towards them. Biggles's face was beaming as he taxied up to the beach and switched off—'so that we shall hear the other machine coming if it's on its way back,' he explained.

Dickpa took over charge of the prisoner while the others went to work with a will at the task of filling the tanks, Smyth standing on the hull while the others fed him with cans of petrol. The empties were thrown back on to the beach, so that they could not damage the hull in taking off, which they might have done had they been allowed to float on the river.

'What is he talking about?' called Biggles once to Dickpa, observing that he and his prisoner were having an animated conversation.

'He is asking me to take him with us. He says the others will kill him when they find the petrol gone.'

'Best thing they could do; it would serve him thundering well right.'

'That's what I've just told him,' replied Dickpa blandly.

It took them more than half an hour of strenuous work to empty the cans, and by the end of that time the tanks were nearly full.

'That's better,' said Biggles approvingly, as he once more took his place in the cockpit. 'I should tie that fellow's hands behind his back,' he advised, nodding towards the prisoner. 'We don't want him taking pot shots at us as we take off.'

The Brazilian's hands were accordingly tied, much to his relief, for he was still nervous that the generous treatment he had received was too good to be true, and was only a preliminary to being put to death.

'Hark!' cried Biggles suddenly, and in the hush that followed, they could faintly hear the hum of the returning flying-boat. 'All aboard,' he cried, and a minute later they were off, circling upwards towards the sun, in the blazing brilliancy of which there would be little chance of their being seen. Far away a tiny point of light flashing in the sky showed them where the other machine was moving. The flashes were caused by the sun's rays striking the wings and struts of the Curtiss as it banked steeply, a manœuvre Biggles was careful to avoid for that very reason.

He flew upstream parallel with the river until the tributary which led to the mountains and the treasure-caves came into view, when he turned off and followed its tortuous course. Algy looked at him and raised his eyebrows, but Biggles's reassuring signal put his mind at rest. A few minutes later he made another signal, this time to take over control, and then he reached for the writing-pad which was kept in the loose canvas pocket inside the cockpit, and wrote rapidly:

'Cannot land on river without being found by the Curtiss. Am going to risk landing on prairie near cave. Will go over first by parachute to clear a runway; will make smoke signal for you to land when ready.'

He passed the note to Algy and held the joystick while he read it. Except for a slight grimace to indicate that he was not enamoured of the plan, but accepted it for want of a better one, he made no comment.

They were now close to the mountains that marked the position of the cave, and Biggles disappeared into the cabin. A moment later he returned with the parachute harness buckled about him. They were flying at about three thousand feet, and he signalled Algy to drop lower, guiding him with his hand, over the course he wished him to fly.

There seemed to be little or no wind, so, provided the parachute opened properly, he was taking no risks in making the jump. They were down to 1,500 feet now, circling over an open space free from boulders, quite close to the cliff. Indeed, the prairie was more or less open as far as he could see, rolling away to the far horizon in long undulations. Here and there groups of buriti palms, in the spinney-like formation common to the region, studded the plain with their dark, feathery foliage and still darker shadows. Biggles raised his arm above his head. Algy throttled back almost to stalling point and saw him leap outwards and down. He breathed a sigh of relief as the silk chute billowed out like a great mushroom and sank slowly earthwards.

Biggles landed safely, and, freeing himself from the parachute harness, set about making a runway for the machine to land. For a good quarter of an hour he worked feverishly, hauling away big stones and branches of trees from the track he was making, but at last he was satisfied that there were no obstacles likely to impede the *Condor*.

Algy, still circling above, saw the smoke of a small fire rise into the still air, and the drone of the engine died away suddenly as he began to glide down towards it. He was not very happy at the responsibility thrust upon him. Normally, of course, he would land almost anywhere without giving the matter a passing thought, but now so much was at stake that he bit his lip in his anxiety. He had little fear of a crash, but while a faulty landing might not do more than shake his passengers, it might easily result in damage to the machine far beyond their power to repair. But his fears were groundless. With his eyes fixed on the track, he flattened out and glided in to a perfect three-point landing. The *Condor* bumped a little as she ran to a stop over the rough ground, but that was unavoidable, and Biggles's reassuring shout of approbation and relief brought a smile to Algy's anxious face. 'Good show,' called Biggles approvingly.

'Which way?' yelled Algy from the cockpit, with the prop still ticking over, knowing that it would not be wise to leave the machine in the broiling sun without some risk of impairing the doped fabric.

'Follow me,' called Biggles, and led the way to a nearby group of buriti palms.

'OK., switch off!' he shouted as they reached them, and the fitful splutter of the engine faded into silence. The door opened and the others alighted.

Dickpa was beaming. 'Now that's what I call good

work!' he cried. 'I couldn't have done it better myself,' he added with a broad grin.

'I'd hate to be with you when you tried,' rejoined Biggles, with a wink at Algy. 'I think we can sit pretty here. Bring an axe, Smyth, and we'll carve a lane into these trees; the shade will protect the machine and Silas & Co. will need better eyes than they've got to spot us. They'll wonder where the dickens we've gone,' he concluded.

Willing hands soon cut a pathway into the heart of the thicket; palm fronds were placed over the planes and on the top of the fuselage until it was perfectly concealed from aerial observation.

Biggles flung his axe down and mopped his perspiring face. 'She'll do,' he said laconically. 'Phew! let's have a rest. I think we've earned one.'

'Yes, I think we have,' agreed Dickpa. 'Well, we can make a comfortable camp here, and stay a month if necessary.'

'I wouldn't mind staying six months if it wasn't for these accursed flies,' muttered Biggles, removing a bee from his ear. 'Give me a pin, someone. I'm being eaten alive by *carrapatosses.*'

Stores were unloaded and they were soon sitting down to the first real meal they had had since their arrival in the Matto Grosso.

'We shall have to be careful with fires,' observed Dickpa. 'You can see smoke for a surprising distance in this atmosphere; it's like crystal, and distance is deceiving. How far away do you suppose that hill is?' he asked pointing to a great mass of rock that stood like an isolated Gibraltar on the far side of the plain.

'Five miles, although it doesn't look more than three,' guessed Algy.

'Ten,' offered Biggles.

'Fifty would be nearer,' observed Dickpa.

'Fifty!'

'Easily that. When you've spent as much time in this country as I have it no longer gives you a shock to find that you can see things distinctly that may take two or three days of really hard going to reach.'

'Well, I'll take your word for it,' murmured Biggles, stretching himself out luxuriously on the ground. He sprang to his feet with a wild yell. 'Drat the ants!' he raved. 'Let's get the hammocks out.'

'I suggest we clear the mouth of the cave first,' said Dickpa. 'We shall then be all ready to march straight in in the morning and begin work on the wall inside.'

'That sounds a good scheme to me,' agreed Biggles. 'Let me see, we left the tools there, didn't we, so we shan't need anything.'

Dickpa entered the machine and returned with a flashlight, which he slipped into his pocket. 'I'm ready,' he announced.

It was not more than a quarter of a mile to the brook where it passed the mouth of the cave, and they found everything just as they had left it. They went to work with a will, occasionally pausing to listen, to make sure they were not caught unawares by the enemy flying-boat. At the end of an hour the cleft in the rock was cleared of debris, and, not without some trepidation, they entered.

'Another fall of rock while we're inside is not a pleasant thing to contemplate,' was Biggles's unspoken thought as he followed the others into the cave.

It was an eerie scene. The beam of the flashlamp stabbed the darkness like a sword and disturbed great bats that wheeled and circled about them, occasionally striking their faces with their leathery wings, much to Algy's disgust. The knowledge, too, that they were treading a path last used by men hundreds of years before produced a queer sensation.

'That's where I found the gold,' said Dickpa, pointing.

'All I can say is, you must have had your nerve with you to come in a spooky place like this alone,' observed Biggles. 'I don't mind how high up above the ground I get, but I'm nothing for going down under it.'

'Pah! It's safer here than in that flimsy contrivance of wood and canvas,' jibed Dickpa.

Biggles made no reply, and for some time they stumbled on over the uneven path, often slipping over small round boulders on the floor. 'By the look of these stones I should say water came down here some time,' resumed Biggles at length.

'It did,' agreed Dickpa. 'The place—the whole country, in fact—was once under the sea. That can be proved in a dozen ways. You'll find shells and fossils everywhere if you look for them, even in the mountains. This cave is a natural one, I am quite certain, and was caused by the rock splitting during some great upheaval in the past. Many of the rock formations in the Matto Grosso are split like this. Well, here we are,' he concluded.

They stopped before what at first looked like the blank end of the cave, but close examination revealed that it was artificial and not natural. Biggles marvelled at the cunning hands that wrought such fine work without the use of either steel or mortar.

'There it is, just as I described it to you at home,' said Dickpa quietly, and with an air that almost amounted to reverence. 'It's too late to start work on it today, I'm afraid. It must be well on in the afternoon, and we are all dead beat. I think we had better get back, make a comfortable camp, and have a real good night's rest. We shall then be able to start fit and fresh first thing in the morning. By this time tomorrow I hope we shall be the other side of the wall.'

Chapter 11
The Ants

Biggles awoke early the following morning and lay for a few minutes contemplating the pink blush of the tropic dawn through a delicate tracery of palm fronds. Then, for some reason which he was unable to determine, a strange feeling began to creep over him that all was not well. His first thought was of the *Condor*, and, turning over in his hammock, he regarded it with relief. There it was, exactly as they had left it. Was it, though? Something seemed changed, but what it was he could not see in the half-light. He swung over the side of the hammock and, slipping on his shoes, hurried towards it, slowing down as he approached nearer, staring.

The exposed portion of the wings and plane surfaces where they showed through the leaves that had been laid on them were black, as if they had had some sticky black substance poured over them, a heavy viscous fluid like tar that was still slowly moving and dripping off the edges. For a full minute he stared at it uncomprehendingly, and then let out a wild yell that brought the others from their hammocks with a rush.

'What is it?' asked Dickpa calmly, his rifle across his arm.

'Look,' replied Biggles in a strangled whisper, pointing at the machine, and then again, 'Look!'

The others looked, or rather gazed spellbound at the incredible sight that confronted them.

'Ants!' ejaculated Dickpa. 'Millions and millions of

them! *Saubas*, too—no, by the great Lord Harry, they're not. They're bigger than *saubas*—a new sort to me. They must have been converging on the *Condor* all night. I wonder what could have attracted them.'

'Dope*,' answered Biggles, 'the dope on the fabric. It's sweet to the taste, I believe; domestic animals have been known to lick the wings of a machine left in a field all night.'

'What are we going to do?' asked Algy at last.

'We've got to do something, and that quickly,' retorted Biggles. 'There won't be any aeroplane left by tonight at the rate they are working.'

'But how,' cried Algy, in something like a panic. 'How on earth are we going to shift 'em?'

Biggles pondered the question. 'We can't just shoo 'em away,' he observed. 'It's no use shouting at 'em and it's no use shooting at 'em; what the dickens *are* we going to do? Come on, Dickpa, it's up to you.'

Dickpa had been busy while they were talking, hurrying round the machine and examining it from every angle. 'I don't know,' he confessed, 'not yet. I've heard of these ants, now I come to think of it. They call them the *sauba grosso*—the big *saubas*, in other words. They sting like the deuce. I believe one single bite can be very painful, and cause considerable discomfort for days.'

'How about smoking them off?' suggested Biggles.

'It might do it, but I doubt it,' replied Dickpa. 'But a smoke cloud big enough to do any good would probably be seen by the enemy, apart from the danger of setting the machine on fire—or the whole prairie, if it comes to that. Starting a fire in this dry stuff near some hundreds of gallons of petrol strikes me as being a highly dangerous performance.'

---

* Liquid similar to varnish, applied to the fabric surfaces to stiffen and weatherproof them.

'How about starting the engine and blowing them off with the slipstream of the prop?' volunteered Smyth, speaking for the first time.

'It might shift some of them, but who's going to start the engine?' asked Biggles promptly.

'I will,' offered Smyth, gallantly starting forward.

'Stand where you are, man, and don't be a fool!' cried Dickpa. 'They'd tear you to pieces. It's impossible, I tell you. Wait a minute; let me think.'

'It looks to me as if every ant in South America is congregating on that kite,' exclaimed Biggles bitterly to Algy, 'and they're still coming; you can see them in the grass if you look, all shapes and sizes. Holy mackerel, look out! Look out, Dickpa!' he yelled suddenly, and dashed to one side. 'Strewth, that's done it,' he groaned.

The others, who had followed in his rush for shelter, now turned to ascertain the cause, and the sight that met their horrified gaze was so unexpected, so terrifying, and so utterly preposterous that for a minute no one moved or spoke. They could only stand and stare with straining eyes.

Across the short scrubby turf, not more than twenty feet away, came what at first sight seemed to be a wide ribbon slowly moving forward, a dark creeping stain like a shadow cast by a cloud on an April day.

'Ants!' gasped Algy in a choking whisper. 'Hundreds of thousands of millions of myriads—and we thought they were all here. I can hear them—hark at them pattering in the grass!' His voice rose to a shrill crescendo and ended in a long, high-pitched laugh.

'Stop that!' cried Dickpa angrily. 'Get hold of yourself—it's nothing to go crazy about.'

What Algy had said was true. A long column of ants was advancing towards the machine, an army that could not be measured in terms of figures. In front of it were small groups that ran to and fro quickly, like skirmishers. They were quite small, not a quarter of the size of their big brothers on the machine, but they were as countless as the sands on a seashore.

'Well, that looks like the end of it to me,' muttered Biggles resignedly. 'We can't destroy that lot except by fire, and then we destroy the machine as well. Would you believe it, eh?' he concluded gloomily, turning to the others.

'No,' declared Dickpa emphatically, 'I wouldn't. I know Brazil pretty well, and I warned you ants existed in enormous numbers, but I've never seen anything like this before. That lot would wipe out a village. I shouldn't do that,' he went on quickly as Smyth took a pace or two towards them and crushed some under his heel.

Instantly, as if directed by some signal, a narrow black column broke off from the main body and advanced upon the intruder. There was something appalling in the deliberate attack. Smyth backed away hurriedly and turned a trifle pale.

'I say,' he muttered hoarsely, 'look at this—look at this! They're attacking the big fellows, fighting like fury!'

The others dashed forward, a ray of hope shining in Dickpa's eyes. 'If they are fighting, it may be the answer to the problem!' he cried excitedly. 'Ants of different sorts fight to the bitter end—murderous wars of extermination.'

'If the little ones win and take possession of the machine, we shall only be out of the frying-pan into the fire,' observed Biggles.

'Not necessarily,' declared Dickpa, 'they might not be the stinging sort, or they might not stay on the

130

machine. It's the other ants they're after—just look at them!'

The truth of his words was soon apparent. There was no doubt that the newcomers were driving the larger ants before them, throwing themselves upon them with tigerish ferocity. In fact, the *saubas* on the ground were already beating a retreat, or, rather, running about aimlessly, sometimes with two or three of the smaller ones hanging on to them. The head of the new column reached the *Condor*, and, like a black stain, began to spread up the outside of the fuselage. Stark panic seized the *saubas*.

'I can't watch it, I'm getting dizzy,' muttered Biggles in an undertone. 'We had better go and see that our things are all right while they are fighting it out. We can't do anything here, that's certain.'

They hurried back to the hammocks and the pile of tinned provisions which they had taken from the machine, but there was no cause for alarm. They were just as they had left them, and not a sign of an ant anywhere.

'I'm glad that first lot decided to go for the machine and not us,' mused Biggles. 'Fancy waking up in the middle of the night to find that lot crawling over you. Pah!'

'Hist! Look!' It was Dickpa's turn to utter a startled exclamation, but it was quickly followed with a smile. 'That fellow knows how to cope with ants better than we do,' he whispered.

'What is it?' breathed Algy, staring at a dark animal with a long snout that had appeared beside the machine.

'Ant-eater—lives on ants—breakfast, lunch, and dinner; look at his tongue. He's got a long strip of a tongue covered with sticky stuff. Usually he sticks it in the ants' nest, and, when it has collected a nice coating of ants, he pulls it out and swallows them. He's having the time of his life there—just look at him. There's another of them, by Jove!'

There was no doubt that the ant-eaters were having a wonderful time among the ants, but even they could make little impression on so great a number.

'I believe the little fellows are driving the *saubas* off alright,' observed Algy excitedly, approaching the machine cautiously.

It was true. Not only were the big ants retiring precipitately, but the smaller ones were following them, passing straight over the machine in their line of march.

'I think we might try to get the *Condor* away now,' said Dickpa. 'The big fellows might come back or another lot come along. If we could get a rope round her tail we might drag her out into the open.'

'Where are we going to put her if we do?' asked Algy.

'In the brook, with her wheels in the water,' replied Biggles quickly. 'That's the only place I can think of, anyway. But there, if we do, I suppose it will be attacked by a swarm of those devilish fish—what did you call them, Dickpa?'

'*Pirhanas*. No, they're not likely to bother it,' laughed Dickpa. 'Come on, then; it will be warm work dragging her across the open, but it can't be helped. I can't think why I overlooked the possibility of ants getting in the machine,' he went on apologetically as they quickly tied the hammock-ropes together into a handy length of line. 'I remember warning you in England that we might be inconvenienced by ants.'

'Inconvenienced!' laughed Biggles. 'You were right there. But I hope they haven't done any damage,' he added, becoming serious.

The tail of the amphibian was neatly lassoed and lifted, and Biggles quickly slipped another line around the tail-skid. 'Haul away, but not too fast!' he shouted, and ran round to the nose of the machine, from where he directed operations, occasionally giving the hull a push where it was clear of ants, for isolated battles were still being waged at various points.

The movement of the machine seemed to expedite their evacuation, however, and a cheer of relief was raised when the last combatants fell, still struggling, to the ground. For nearly an hour the airmen toiled and sweltered in the heat, for the sun was now well up, before they reached the bank of the stream at its nearest point, which was only a few hundred yards from the place where it skirted the cliff in which the cave was situated.

'Steady now!' called Biggles, taking a spade from the cabin and clearing a smooth wheel-track down to the water, which was not more than a few inches deep. A few shrubs and saplings had to be cleared to allow the wide wing span of the *Condor* to pass, and then the big machine was allowed to glide gently down into the water, where it was turned facing the current, the water just lapping around the bottom of the fuselage.

'We had better cut some small stuff and cover the wings, like we did before,' suggested Biggles. 'It's quite on the boards that the other crowd may come this way looking for us, and we can't afford to risk them seeing her. Luckily they've only got a flying-boat, so they couldn't land here, anyway, but if they saw her they would probably march overland. That will do, I think,' he went on a few minutes later, when the wings and tail had been well strewn with reeds and small branches. 'She ought to be safe here—if there is such a thing as a safe place in Brazil,' he added, with a sly glance at Dickpa.

'There isn't,' was the old explorer's frank reply.

'That's what I was beginning to think,' retorted Biggles, grinning. 'Well, let's have a bit of breakfast. I think we've earned it.'

'Yes, let's get on with it,' agreed Dickpa. 'I was hoping yesterday that we should be behind the wall in the cave by this time today.'

'It doesn't do to hope too much in the Matto Grosso,' observed Biggles, with his mouth full of biscuit. 'The only thing I have yet seen in Brazil that is any good is this,' he went on, indicating a mug of steaming coffee at his side. 'I must say they grow pretty good coffee; but, now I come to think of it, I haven't seen any Brazil nuts. Somewhere in the back of my mind I had an idea that Brazil nuts came from Brazil.'

'Ha, ha!' laughed Dickpa.

'Well, they do, don't they?' protested Biggles.

'Of course, but not in this part, and you don't pick them like filberts, you know; but come on, we're wasting time.'

The cooking and eating utensils were soon cleaned in the sand on the bank of the stream, and stowed away in the cabin. Water-bottles were filled and haversacks stuffed with food and articles likely to be of service in the cave, such as a flashlight, matches, and so on. Just as they were leaving, Biggles untied the rope that was still tied to the *Condor's* tail-skid, and, coiling it neatly, threw it over his shoulder. 'I think I'll bring this along; it may come in handy,' he observed casually.

In such simple actions does Fate show her hand.

With cheerful smiles and the thrill of the treasure-hunt upon them, they strode off gaily in the direction of the cave.

Chapter 12
Trapped

They found the tools and the entrance of the cave exactly as they had left them, so they were able to make their way without delay to the face of the wall that barred their progress. On reaching it, Dickpa balanced the flashlight on a stone in such a manner that its rays were directed on the middle of the wall, and Biggles, placing his haversack and water-bottle on the ground behind them, picked up a hammer and cold chisel.

'What do you think is the best way of setting about it?' he asked Dickpa in perplexity, examining the smooth face of the wall closely. 'I wish I knew how thick it was.'

'We shall just have to chisel away until we get one stone out; after that it should be possible to prise the others out. We needn't pull the whole wall down; all we need is a hole big enough to crawl through,' observed Dickpa.

Biggles set to work with a will, and at the end of ten minutes had succeeded in making a good-sized concave hole in the centre stone. He handed the tools to Algy with a, 'Carry on; it's warm work,' and Algy, flinging his jacket aside, proceeded with the task. Suddenly he paused in the middle of a stroke and stepped back hastily.

'What's wrong?' asked Biggles with some concern.

'I don't quite know,' muttered Algy. 'I don't know whether it's because I'm getting giddy in the dark, but

135

I thought I felt the whole wall quiver, as if it was being shaken. Oh, lor', I'm going to be sick. I'm giddy.' With his arm resting on the wall, he turned to stare at Biggles, who had staggered and nearly measured his length on the floor.

A dull murmur, like distant thunder, reached their ears and brought Biggles to his feet with a rush. 'What is it?' he gasped.

At the first sound Dickpa had leapt for the flashlight. 'Quick,' he snapped, as the floor of the cave sagged sickeningly. 'Get out—it's an earthquake! Ah—stop!' he screamed.

There came a deafening roar from somewhere down the tunnel up which they had come, and the air was filled with a cloud of choking, blinding dust. The sides of the cave quivered like jelly, and a few pieces of rock fell from the roof with a crash; then all was still again.

Dickpa was still holding the flashlight. 'Stand where you are,' he said in a dull voice, and disappeared into the darkness. He was back almost at once. 'The whole tunnel has caved in,' was all he said, and then sat down on the floor.

It was some time before anyone spoke. Then, 'I suppose there's no chance of breaking through?' said Biggles in a strained voice.

'None whatever. The whole roof has closed down on to the floor,' replied Dickpa quietly.

There was another long silence, which was broken by Algy. 'How long do you think the air in here will last?' he said in a curiously calm voice.

'There's no telling; a few hours at the most, I should think,' came Dickpa's voice from behind the flashlamp.

'Well, let's do something,' exclaimed Biggles irritably, picking up the hammer and chisel that Algy had dropped. 'It's no use just sitting here—we shall all go crazy.' He flung himself upon the wall in a fury, cutting out pieces from the central stone, regardless of the chips that flew in all directions.

'There doesn't seem to be much object—' began Dickpa, but Biggles cut him short.

'I always try to finish what I start. I came here to see Mr. Atta-somebody's treasure. Alright; my motto is, "Atta boy" while I have the strength to stand up.'

'I'm very sorry about this,' began Dickpa again.

Biggles threw the tools down and crossed over to him quickly. 'I know how you feel, Dickpa,' he said gently. 'You're blaming yourself for getting us in this mess. Well, don't. We came on this show with our eyes wide open, all of us, Algy, Smyth, and myself, the same as we've done all the other shows we've been on. We've been in tight corners before today. Many's the time I've said to myself, "Biggles, you're a goner," but I've got away with it every time up to now. There may be another earthquake any minute which will open the cave again. Anything can happen in Brazil—you've said it yourself. Anyway, whatever happens, don't blame yourself unless you want us all to sit down and bleat—that's right, isn't it, Algy?'

'Absolutely,' replied Algy instantly.

Biggles picked up the tools and again attacked the wall, whistling cheerfully between strokes. Perspiration poured from his face, but still he worked on.

'Here, let me have a go,' said Algy, who was watching him.

'You start on a hole of your own if you want one. This one's mine,' grinned Biggles, with a gallant attempt at humour that deceived no one.

The time passed on leaden wings, and Biggles's strokes became slower and weaker. 'Getting warmish,' he observed, after a long silence.

No one answered. They knew the air in their living tomb was rapidly becoming vitiated. The oxygen was nearly exhausted. Biggles stopped work and leaned against the wall, nearly spent, his breath coming in short gasps. He saw that Dickpa had fallen against the side of the cave; Smyth was on his knees, struggling for breath. Turning, he scowled at the hole he had made in the wall. 'Beaten me after all, have you?' he gritted through his teeth. 'Well, hold that!' and he flung the hammer at it with all his might in a fit of fighting rage.

The hammer disappeared from sight; there was a slight clatter as it fell some distance away out of sight. For a moment Biggles stared unbelievingly, and then leapt at the wall, groping frantically for the hole that he knew must be there. A current of cool, sweet air poured over his streaming face like a draught of cold water. His shrill yell, 'Air,' aroused Algy from his lethargy, and, reeling unsteadily, he staggered to the hole and swallowed deep gasping mouthfuls of the life-giving oxygen. Then he helped Biggles to get Dickpa toward the hole, but the fresh air had already flooded the chamber and Dickpa opened his eyes before they reached it. 'What is it?' he said feebly.

'We've struck air.'

'Air?'

'Yes, I busted through the wall at the last moment and fresh air is coming in from the other side of it. Whether it is just a supply that was there before the cave fell in, or whether there is an opening somewhere ahead, remains to be seen, but it gives us another chance. We've got to get a hole in that wall big enough to get through. Have a go at it, Algy,' he concluded, turning his hands palms outwards towards the light.

An exclamation of sympathy broke from the lips of

the others, for Biggles's hands, which were small and delicate, were now blistered and raw as a result of his labour at the wall. 'Funny, funny, and I never even noticed it,' he laughed. 'It's queer how minor hurts cease to matter when one is faced with a big one. That's the stuff, boy.'

This last remark was addressed to Algy, who had picked up the chisel, and, under the impetus of renewed hope, set about enlarging the hole, hacking savagely at the edges. Smyth, too, had picked up a steel mooring-pin that they had brought with them and was prising away at the corners. But the wall, as Dickpa had pointed out, was a work of art, each block of stone having been cut to fit the aperture for which it was intended, and even then appeared to have been literally 'ground in,' like the valve of an engine, so perfectly did it fit. It was about two feet in thickness, but it slowly succumbed to the onslaught of the fresh attack. Two more stones were dislodged after having been partly hewn away, and Dickpa called a halt, pointing out that the breach was now large enough to admit them.

Biggles put his head and shoulders through the hole and stared into the pitch blackness. 'Pass me the flash-light,' he said.

'Well, what can you see?' asked Dickpa impatiently, for the others were unable to reach the hole, which Biggles's body almost filled.

'Nothing,' came the disappointed answer. 'Not a blooming thing—except rock; and there's plenty of that.'

'What?' exclaimed Dickpa incredulously. 'Nothing?'

'There's no treasure, if that's what you mean, but it looks as if the cave goes right on, which is something, anyway. Pass the tools and things along. We can't go back, so we've no choice but to go forward.'

Biggles disappeared through the hole, and, after the tools and equipment had been handed through, the others joined him. They found that the cave widened considerably behind the wall, as if it had been enlarged by human hands.

'It certainly looks as if we've drawn a blank,' observed Dickpa. ' "And when they got there the cupboard was bare," so to speak,' he quoted sadly. 'I must confess I am very disappointed; not that it seems to matter very much now. The treasure wouldn't be much good to us even if we found it. Well, it isn't here, so that's the end of it.'

'I don't know so much,' replied Biggles slowly. He was running his hands carefully over the inside of the wall, and presently he struck a match and peered closely at it. 'Now *I'll* tell you something,' he muttered in a voice that trembled slightly. 'This wall wasn't built from the other side at all—I mean the way we came in. It was built from *this* side. This wall was built because the priests—or whoever they were—knew about the back door that opened on to the stream and they decided to block it up. They probably went down there for fresh air and water while they were building. That's about it,' he went on excitedly. 'It was on such an occasion that some silly ass amused himself by doing a little rock-carving practice, or maybe it wasn't just carelessness after all. The fellow concerned might have had an idea at the back of his mind of coming round to the back door when the job was done and helping himself to the odd spot of gold. That's just the sort of thing some crafty priest might have done. There are all sorts of clefts and caves in these mountains—at least, so you've told us—so naturally it would be a wise precaution to mark the only one that really mattered.'

'And it looks as if some scrimshanker was already

pilfering the treasure,' suggested Dickpa. 'He must have dropped that piece of gold I found. But do you realize what it means?'

'Of course I do,' broke in Biggles. 'It means that the people who built the wall must have gone out the way they came. In other words, there is a way out into the open air somewhere ahead up the cave, and that's about as much as I'm concerned with at the moment. Once let me clap my peepers on blue sky again, and I shall think twice before I start burrowing underground again. I'm no mole.'

'You're dead right about the wall!' exclaimed Dickpa, who was examining it minutely in the beam of the flashlamp and comparing it with the other side. 'The joints are not quite so close. The rocks are cut slightly wedge-shape and then driven in like a plug in a barrel. No wonder it was air-tight.'

'That's what I thought,' agreed Biggles. 'But dash the wall! I've seen enough of it. Let's get a move on and see where the cave leads to. I'm pining to see the sky again.'

They picked up their bags, and, with Biggles leading the way with the flashlight, they filed up the narrow passage.

'Hullo, what's this?' he cried suddenly, after they had gone a short distance. 'Steps, by James, steps! What do you know about that? It strikes me that this might still be the way to Attaboy's old oak chest!'

'Atahuallpha,' snapped Dickpa irritably.

But Biggles wasn't listening. He gave a grunt of disappointment as the short flight of steps ended abruptly and they found themselves in a similar passage to the one below. They went on slowly, and presently came to more steps.

'Phew!' muttered Biggles, when they reached the top

and saw the tunnel stretching away in front of them again. 'I must have a drink; this is heavy going.'

'You notice that we are going up all the time?' Dickpa pointed out. 'The floor of the cave slopes upwards all the way. It looks to me as if they cut these steps at the most difficult places— where there was a sudden drop—to save using ropes.'

'It looks that way to me,' agreed Biggles, as they again resumed their march.

The cave seemed interminable. In places the ceiling was so high that the flashlight failed to reveal the roof, and at others it was so low that they had to stoop to pass. Steps occurred frequently; sometimes only two or three, sometimes twenty or more, and on one occasion there were so many that they lost count. And all the time the floor of the cave rose steeply upwards. In one place, however, Biggles nearly had a nasty fall, for there was a sudden unexpected flight of steep steps leading downwards, and he only saw them just as he was stepping off into space.

'Here, my lad, you had better have a rope round you,' cautioned Dickpa. 'Algy, pass that rope along; this is no place for somebody to break a leg.'

Biggles at first protested, but finally submitted to being tied round the waist with the rope they had brought with them, and they proceeded with Algy holding the other end. A few minutes later, Algy, who wanted to use both hands to manipulate his water-bottle, carelessly tied the rope around his own waist. They stopped at a fairly wide part of the cave to eat some food and take a rest, for the atmosphere was heavy and they were all nearly exhausted. They had lost all count of time and distance. Indeed, as Algy remarked, they seemed to have been walking along the passage not merely a matter of hours, but of days.

The upward incline of the floor became even steeper soon after they had resumed their march, and all of them were soon feeling the strain.

'Never mind, it's a long lane that has no turning,' panted Algy.

'This must be the one the fellow who said that was thinking of,' gasped Biggles. 'Look—!' He broke off short with a sharp yell of fright. What came next occurred so suddenly that for a moment or two Algy could not think what had happened. He heard Biggles's startled cry and then he was whipped off his feet, knocking Dickpa sprawling as he fell. An invisible hand seemed to be dragging him along the floor of the cave. He grunted as Smyth flung himself upon him and the motion stopped. He raised his eyes, and then shuddered as he found himself staring into space. It was quite dark, but the sky was ablaze with stars. Then, as his muddled faculties began to work again, he looked down and saw Biggles about twenty feet below, dangling on the end of the rope over a sheer chasm, the bottom of which was lost in Stygian blackness. He was turning round slowly, like a joint on a spit, and then his voice came floating up to them.

'Hi!' he called, staring up into Algy's startled face. 'Haul me up—the rope's going! Make haste!'

Algy felt Dickpa's body kneeling beside him, and heard his swift, concise instructions.

'Haul steadily, everybody, when I give the word. Smyth, slip your coat under the rope where it chafes on the edge of the cliff or the rock will cut it like a piece of cotton. Algy, crawl backwards as we heave, and hang on to anything you can reach; if he starts slipping, you'll both go. Now!' he yelled.

Then followed a period of pulling and struggling, which to Algy seemed like a horrid nightmare from which he could not awake. From some distance down the cave he saw Biggles's face appear over the edge of the cliff; there was a quick scuffle, punctuated with gasps and grunts, and then Biggles fell headlong into the cave, where he lay breathing heavily.

Algy, when the tension on the rope relaxed, sank limply to the floor; blood was running down his face from a nasty cut in his forehead, and his whole body ached with bruises from the battering it had received.

'Why the dickens don't you look where you're going?' he snarled when he could get his breath.

'If you think—I just—leapt—into space—for fun— you're wrong,' panted Biggles furiously. 'Holy mackerel! Brazil—where the nuts come from. Bah! where the mutts *go to* would be nearer the mark. What about a nice quiet evening listening in or something for a change? Where are we, anyway?'

'Don't try and be funny,' growled Algy.

'Funny! Ha, ha! If you think it's funny hanging suspended over nothing on a piece of string, you have a go at it. I'm no spider.'

'Well, you said you wanted to see the sky; now you've seen it. What are you grumbling about? There it is,' concluded Algy airily, pointing towards the opening of the cave.

'You went out so fast that you thundering nearly missed seeing it altogether,' observed Dickpa, who was lying at full length on the brink of the cliff cautiously trying to see if he could find a continuation of the path. 'I can't see anything except cliff,' he went on. 'We shall have to sit still and wait for daylight before we do anything else.'

'That suits me remarkably well,' agreed Biggles. 'I've had all the mountain climbing I want for one day. How often do they have earthquakes here?'

'Why?'

'I should hate another to come along and pitch us out of that hole,' replied Biggles. 'Has anyone got the time?'

'You busted my watch when you slid out of the window,' stated Algy.

'And I forgot to wind mine up,' announced Dickpa, 'but, judging by the position of the Southern Cross,* I should say it's well after midnight.'

'Roll on, morning,' murmured Biggles, settling himself down at full length and using a haversack for a pillow.

*The pole star of the Southern Hemisphere.

Chapter 13

Marooned

They dozed fitfully on and off until a grey tinge, slowly turning to pink, diffused the sky. Presently a shaft of brilliant light caught a projecting ledge of rock, causing it to glow like a living flame.

'Oh,' groaned Biggles, sitting up and stretching stiffly. 'Let us have a look-see,' he mumbled, crawling on all fours towards the oval-shaped section of light that marked the entrance—or rather the exit—of the cave. Lying flat on his stomach, he looked out over the edge, and the sight that met his gaze was so stupendous that in spite of their predicament he uttered a low cry of admiration.

In front of them, level with their eyes, stretched an array of minarets of red rock, the tops glowing like points of orange fire in the light of the rising sun. Between them were deep wells of cold blue shadows in which soft, downy billows of mist hung motionless. Immediately below was a vast crater, the bottom of which was hidden under a curtain of purple shade, so profound and intense that it seemed possible to reach out and touch it. Biggles caught his breath as he stared unbelievingly. The scene was unreal, fantastic, as if they were looking at another world. A slight movement made him look up, and he half smiled when he saw the others crowding behind him, lost in wonderment at the glorious panorama. Something above, and slightly to one side, caught his eye, and his sharp

146

ejaculation brought Dickpa forward, trying to ascertain the cause of it.

'Steps!' said Biggles tensely. 'This *is* a way out after all, but, by the anti-clockwise propeller of my sainted aunt, it is a staircase that I, for one, am not anxious to tread. I don't mind looking down when I've got a couple of wings each side of me, but it is going to be heady work scaling that crazy gangway.'

'Can you see where it leads to, or how far it extends?' asked Algy curiously.

'No—hold my feet in case I slip—that's right. The steps start about half way up the side of the cave and wind round out of sight somewhere over the top. Well, wherever they lead to, we've got to follow them, but I don't mind admitting that we've got a bit too high up in the world for my liking. Who's going first?'

'I'll go,' offered Dickpa promptly.

'No, I'll go,' returned Biggles decisively. 'I'm the lightest. I'll rope myself up again, and you can brace yourself to take the strain of my fall in case I slip or the steps break down. I'll tell you what it's like as I go, and then you will know what to expect.'

Without further ado, he fastened the rope tightly about his waist and, seizing a projecting crag, swung himself outwards and up. He was lost to sight instantly, and a short silence followed. A piece of rock bounced down, struck the lip of the cave, and bounded away into space; instinctively Algy listened for it to strike the bottom, but it might have fallen into a bottomless pit for all the noise it made.

'Hullo, there!' came Biggles's voice from what seemed to be a great distance away. 'Can you hear me?'

'Can — you — hear — me — you — hear — me — hear —

me,' rang the echoes, becoming fainter and fainter in the distance.

Dickpa cupped his hands around his mouth. 'Yes!' he answered.

'Yes—yes—yes,' came the echoes.

'Dash those echoes,' snarled Algy. 'They give me the creeps.'

'Listen,' came Biggles's voice again. 'I'm at the end of the rope. Let it go. You can follow—it's quite safe—but don't look down. Come one at a time, because there is some loose rock about and someone might get a crack on the head. Bring the haversacks and what tools you can.'

'I'm coming!' shouted Algy, and rose to his feet. His face was rather pale as he seized the crag, swung outwards, and reached with his feet for the bottom step of the dizzy stairway. Following Biggles's instructions, he did not look down, but kept his eyes fixed upwards. At first he could only see a long, curving line of steps that disappeared against the skyline above a rounded dome of rock, but as it mounted higher he saw that it led to a wide open space, with a large pyramid-shaped hill beyond. Biggles was sitting comfortably on a large square stone at the end of the stairway.

Algy joined him breathlessly. 'By the bones of Icarus,' he muttered, 'I may be what the newspapers describe as a birdman, but I'm no steeple-jack; I wouldn't go *down* that path for something.'

Biggles grinned. 'Nor I,' he said, 'not if a dozen Attaboys' treasures were at the bottom'; and then, raising his voice, 'Come on, the next!' he called.

Presently Smyth's head appeared above the top of the rock and the mechanic threw himself down with a sigh of relief. 'Blimey,' he murmured, 'what's our ceiling* at this game? We've got a bit too much altitude for my liking, and the sooner we throttle back and lose a bit of it the better I shall be pleased.'

Biggles laughed. 'You're not the only one,' he said. 'Come on, Dickpa.'

Dickpa, with his haversack held in his teeth, clambered over the brow of the cliff and sank down beside them. 'You were moaning for the blue sky a little while ago, Biggles. Well, now you can see it—all of it,' he observed, looking around at the scene of colossal grandeur. 'Hullo, what are you sitting on?' he went on quickly, noticing the rock on which Biggles was seated. He examined it closely, but it revealed nothing of particular interest, and he turned again to look at the place to which they had ascended.

It was an open plateau about two miles long by a mile wide with a surface of flat rock in most places, but here and there a few stunted trees and bushes eked out a precarious existence in fissures that had been filled up with earth by the wind. Above them, on the far side of the plateau, towered the pyramid-shaped rock. It was clear that they were on the summit of one of the huge flat-topped masses of rock that are such a common feature in the Matto Grosso, and which had been caused, as Dickpa explained, by the subsidence of the surrounding earth, and not by the upheaval of the rock itself. 'The plateau was at one time level with the surrounding country,' he went on. 'You see, it's all volcanic; the colour of the rock tells you that. At some time in the past it has been subjected to terrific heat, perhaps more than once—but come on, let us walk round and see if we can locate ourselves or find a way down.'

---

* The top height to which a plane can fly.

They set off at a steady pace along the edge of the cliff, and soon discovered they were overlooking the mountains on the opposite side of the cliff from where they had entered the cave. In several places the neighbouring peaks were only a short distance away—so close, in fact, that Algy was once able to throw a stone over the intervening abyss. But everywhere the cliff dropped absolutely perpendicularly, sometimes only a few hundred feet, but more often, two or three thousand feet, but in either case it was the same as far as they were concerned. There was not a single place where there was even a remote hope of getting down; no living creature could descend the precipitous wall. They had traversed more than half the circumference of the plateau, and were just beginning to abandon hope—for they knew there was no possible way down on the opposite side, except through the cave, which was now effectually blocked—when Biggles, who had hurried on ahead, uttered a wild 'Whoop' which brought the others on at a run. They joined him, and looked eagerly at a huge buttress of rock which jutted out some distance ahead, at about their own height, and seemed to be a sort of offset from one of the nearby mountains. It appeared to reach the plateau, but for some minutes they were unable to determine whether or not it did actually join up. In his impatience to find out, Biggles threw himself down near the edge of the cliff and peered along the side of it.

He was on his feet again immediately. 'Nothing doing,' he said shortly, concealing his disappointment with difficulty, 'It doesn't quite reach; I can see daylight between.'

They marched on in melancholy silence, for it began to look as if they had escaped death in one form only to meet it in another.

'I've heard of people being marooned at sea, but never on land,' Biggles went on a few moments later, 'and the funny part of it is, I could land an aeroplane up here quite easily—in fact, it looks like a ready-made aerodrome. A machine taking off wouldn't have to climb for height; she'd just take off level and she'd have all the height she wanted right away. Well, we're up here and the plane's at the bottom, so it's no use talking about it, I suppose,' he concluded gloomily.

But Dickpa was not listening. He had suddenly increased his pace, and then pulled up dead in his tracks. A low whistle escaped his lips. The others joined him, and stared in amazement at the sight which met their eyes.

'You've told us many times, Dickpa, that anything can happen in Brazil,' said Biggles, 'but I'm dashed if I expected to find anything like this. It looks as if we've found the front door.'

The object which riveted their attention would not have been remarkable in different circumstances, but it was the last thing any of them expected to find up there. While they were talking they had approached the giant buttress and actually reached it before they were aware that a bridge, about thirty feet wide, spanned the chasm at its narrowest point. It was formed of two whole, roughly squared up trees, laid side by side, without handrails or anything to prevent a careless traveller from stepping straight off into space. To make matters more difficult, one of the trees had slipped, so that it was lower at one end than at the other, and in fact only just resting lightly on the opposite cliff. It looked as if some convulsion of the earth had made the gap wider than it had been originally, for even the second tree only just reached the opposite side and looked as if a good push would send it off altogether.

151

Biggles looked at Dickpa reproachfully.

'I hope you're not going to tell me that I've got to walk across that thing,' he said slowly.

Dickpa shrugged his shoulders. 'It looks as if it's either that or stay here,' he said tersely. 'Who's going first?'

'Wait a minute, wait a minute,' exclaimed Biggles, 'I don't get the hang of all this. Here is a way up to the plateau, that's plain enough, and there was a way down via the cave. You don't tell me that people came across the mountains and across this crazy bridge just for the pleasure of going down again? No, they came up here for something, and it would have to be something pretty important to bring me up here. It looks to me as if this was the main entrance, and one that could be pretty easily closed, too.'

'I believe you're right,' said Dickpa, thinking hard. 'It would be interesting to know what they came up here for.'

'It would, but, not being a soothsayer, thought-reader, or what-not, I can't tell you. Does that look like a track across there, or do I imagine it?'

The others followed his eyes, and saw a rough suggestion of a path leading right across the middle of the plateau on which they stood to the hill on the far side.

'Yes, that's a path alright,' ejaculated Dickpa.

'Very well,' said Biggles simply. 'Don't you think it would be a good thing to see where it leads to before we walk the plank? Since we started I've been shot at, shaken, scared stiff, bitten, stung, hung, buried alive, and goodness knows what else, so I for one am going to have a last look for what we came for. What say you, Algy?'

'Every time,' agreed Algy warmly.

'How about you, Dickpa?'

'Of course.'

'And you, Smyth?'

'Tails up with me,' cried the mechanic, falling back on the old RFC* slogan.

'Come on, then!' cried Biggles enthusiastically, and set off at a fast pace across the plateau, following the old trail which led from the bridge to the pyramid-like mass of rock on the far side.

Its outline grew more rugged as they approached, and it had lost all resemblance to a pyramid by the time they reached its base. It proved to be, in fact, nothing more or less than a huge conglomeration of rock, roughly oval in shape, with a large crown-like peak at one end and a smaller crest at the other. Three sides of it sloped down steeply to the plateau, but the other, which they could not reach, seemed to fall to the sheer lip of the precipice. The trail did not lead straight up, but wound around the hill corkscrew fashion, and was by no means easy to follow. They crossed a small stone bridge over a ravine, and often ascended short flights of steps that had been cut in the most difficult places.

It was now past midday, and the sun blazed down with fierce intensity, but, mopping their faces, they kept on. When they were about three-quarters of the way up, the reason for the winding of the trail became more apparent, for the sides of the hill sloped at such a steep angle in many places that it would have been difficult, if not impossible, to reach the summit by a straight path.

Biggles, in his excitement, was well ahead of the others. They watched him break into a run up the last

* Royal Flying Corps, the forerunner of the RAF.

few yards and then stop with a jerk, at the same time throwing up his hands and staring downwards. For several seconds he remained thus; then he turned and beckoned frantically.

'He's found something,' grunted Dickpa, and redoubled his efforts, all troubles forgotten.

Biggles started down to meet them.

'What is it?' called Dickpa, excited, while they were still some way off.

'I'll give you two guesses!' shouted Biggles.

'*What is it?*' repeated Dickpa, half angry at the delay.

'A town.'

'A *what*?'

'*Town!*'

'Town!'

'Yes, town. T-o-w-n. In other words, a concentration of dwelling-houses, churches, squares, streets, and what-nots.'

'You're joking.'

'Joking my eye! Take a look,' invited Biggles.

Dickpa, with the others at his heels, reached the crest of the hill. Before them lay a deep depression. The whole centre of the hill was, in fact, hollow, as if it had been scooped out with a giant ladle, and they knew they were gazing down into the crater of a long-extinct volcano. But whereas the outside of the eminence was dead rock, gaunt and stark, and devoid of life, the inside presented a picture of sylvan beauty that was almost overwhelming in its unexpected loveliness. It was richly, gloriously green, with a mantle of luxurious grasses and ferns, from which sprang trees and shrubs, many of which were laden with golden or rose-tinted blossoms. So unprepared were the watchers on the rim for such a spectacle that they could only stand and stare, lost in breathless wonder.

154

But that was not all. From the centre, the sides of the crater sloped back in a series of artificial terraces of perfect symmetry. On these were rows of low, square houses, each isolated from, yet identical, with its neighbours, and all facing in the same direction, towards where a tall colonnaded building of Grecian beauty crowned the head of such a flight of steps as they had never seen before and could not have imagined. The whole effect was beautiful beyond description.

Dickpa, at the moment his eyes had rested upon it, had turned as pale as death, and even Biggles, hardened almost to brutality by the careless hand of war, felt a sudden tightening of the heart-strings, while a queer emotion stole over him that the thing was unreal, a hallucination that would presently be dispelled. He glanced at his uncle, whose lips were moving inarticulately, as if he were trying to speak, but could not find words to begin.

Then, 'Let's go down,' said Dickpa, in a strange tone of voice. 'You boys must realise what this means to me,' he went on slowly. 'I've been searching all my life hoping to find something, but I could visualize nothing on such a scale as this. It is the greatest moment of my life, for, unless I am mistaken, this is the biggest discovery of the age, greater perhaps than the discovery of the tomb of Tutankhamen.'

'How do we get down?' muttered Biggles in a strained voice, looking to right and left. 'Ah, here we are,' he went on triumphantly, pointing to a narrow path, which, cut in the rock, wound downwards around the inside face of the cliff. Again the defensive value of the approach, down which only one person could pass at a time, was apparent; a false step would have precipitated a walker on to the house-tops three hundred feet below.

As they drew nearer they could see that most of the buildings were in ruins; trees and shrubs had sprung up within them, and forced their way through the unglazed windows and flat roofs, across which sprawled a tangled growth of vines.

They reached the first dwelling and stopped to look inside. It was clear at first glance that death, swift and unexpected, had overtaken the occupant, for his remains, half mummified in the rare atmosphere, had sunk forward over a bench on which were still scattered the tools of his trade, which had evidently been that of a goldsmith or jeweller, for several exquisitely carved ornaments of the precious metal stood before him; another, half finished, was still clasped between his bony fingers. Two earthenware pots, one containing Indian corn and the other a thick, dark-brown stain that might have once been honey, stood against the wall near his side.

Dickpa picked up one of the ornaments, a carved figure of a llama, looked at it steadfastly for a moment, and then replaced it almost reverently. Not a word was spoken as they emerged into the sunlight again. They entered the next house, and the picture was the same, except that the occupant had evidently been a scribe, for a long pointed instrument and some blocks of stone on which he had been carving lay beside his lifeless body, just as they had fallen from his nerveless grasp when the cold hand of death had struck him down.

In every house they visited, the same pitiful sight met their sympathetic gaze, and, overawed by the atmosphere of tragedy and decay that seemed to pervade the very air, the little party slowly reached the foot of the path.

'Did you notice anything—peculiar—about the—

people—we have seen?' whispered Dickpa, for speech seemed like sacrilege in such a place.

Biggles looked up questioningly. 'No,' he said. 'What—'

'They were all men; we didn't see a single body of a woman.'

'You mean they were—'

'Priests. This wasn't an ordinary town. It must have been a colony of religious devotees or something of the sort. There are years of research work to be done here, many years—but let us go on,' he broke off abruptly, and led the way along a broad, beautifully paved path, still as perfect as the day it was laid, towards the building on the steps that had evidently been a temple. Not until they reached the foot of it did they fully realise its immensity. It seemed to tower far above the rim of the crater, but this they knew was not actually the case. Like flies crawling up a sloping wall they mounted the majestic stairway, a stairway more wonderful than graced the palace of any European king.

It was hard work, for the sun beat down with merciless intensity upon the stone, which reflected a glare which half blinded them with its fierce heat. Weary, and panting for breath, they reached the top and looked about them.

'The sacrificial stone,' said Dickpa shortly, pointing to a great square mass that stood before the entrance of the temple. Its sides were still discoloured with dark significant stains that even the destroying hand of Time had been unable to remove. They reached it in a few strides. On it lay a long, curved knife of unusual material, which Dickpa told them was obsidian, a glass-like, volcanic product. 'These people were sun worshippers,' he went on in a hushed undertone, 'and this is where they carried out their inhuman sacrificial rites that were the one real blot on their otherwise magnificent culture and civilization. But let us go in. We must see as much as we can now we are here, but we cannot stay too late. I am not nervous, but I don't fancy the idea of spending the night here.'

They entered the frowning portal across the wind-scattered bones of one who may have been a sentry, and found themselves in a large, square chamber. After the glare outside, it seemed almost dark, for there were no windows, and instinctively they huddled up closer together in the eerie half-light as they looked about them curiously. Except for a few bodies, one of which wore a magnificent shimmering robe of tiny, bright-hued feathers, woven as tightly as those on the breast of a living bird, the room was empty. A layer of fine dust spread over everything; it rose in clouds under their feet and filled the air with gritty particles that set them coughing and sneezing as they started towards a low, square doorway in the opposite wall.

Chapter 14
Discovery

They crossed the Hall of Doom, as Biggles aptly named the place, and found themselves in another large chamber. It was even larger but darker than the first, for there was no external door and the only light came from two small slits high up in a thick wall. When their eyes became accustomed to the gloom, they perceived only the same grim spectacle of recumbent bodies from which the spirits had long departed. The dust on the floor was deeper; here and there it had drifted into miniature dunes, like sand in the desert, where the wind had ruffled it. Dickpa picked up a handful and looked at it closely.

'Ash,' he said laconically. 'Volcanic ash. But these poor souls were not overwhelmed by an eruption such as overtook the ill-fated city of Pompeii. Pompeii was literally buried under ashes and lava. These unfortunate fellows haven't been burnt, that is quite clear, or their clothes would show it. Yet how did they die? What frightful agent of death could have struck them down wholesale, like the firstborn in Egypt?' He bent over one of the bodies. 'They might have been gassed,' he went on slowly, answering his own question. 'Yes, that was it. Gassed. Choked to death, suffocated by sulphur fumes forced up by some subterranean disturbance such as the one that overtook us in the cave, but much worse. Yes, that must have been it; at least I can think of no other solution.'

'Can't you picture the scene?' he continued in a

voice which betrayed his emotion. 'The priests at their devotions in the temple, on the very spot where we now stand; the lay brothers in their houses on the terraces, all going about their daily tasks with no thought or warning of the impending doom that was about to overtake them; the invincible sword which was to strike them down, from High Priest to the lowest labourer, sparing none. Then, like that'—he clicked his fingers—'the terrifying rumble of unseen forces beneath their feet, a long pulsating quiver, and the silent advance of the gas released by the inferno that was to snuff them out like the firstborn of Egypt.' Dickpa paused, almost overcome by the tragic picture he had portrayed.

'It may have been the same shock that loosened the bridge,' said Biggles quietly.

'Probably, probably,' agreed Dickpa. 'Well, well, it's very sad. But what have we here?' he went on, walking slowly towards a fallen heap of masonry above which yawned a gaping breech in the opposite wall. 'It looks as if it had once been a walled-up doorway which has been shaken down by an earthquake at some time or other. I can see daylight coming in on the far side, too; there must be another outside door, or a large window.'

Side by side they walked across and looked through the gaping hole in the wall. For a long while nobody spoke. Nobody moved, or even seemed to breathe.

Biggles was the first to break the silence, with a long-drawn intake of breath. 'Well, there she is,' he said simply.

Dickpa did not answer. He stood with his left hand resting against the broken wall, staring dully at something that lay beyond, as rigid as if he had been a figure carved in stone.

'Looks like money for jam, sir,' ventured Smyth nervously.

Biggles and Algy started to laugh, but stopped abruptly. Still Dickpa did not speak.

'Well, Dickpa,' said Biggles, nudging him gently, 'is it the treasure or isn't it? Pull yourself together or you'll get fixed in that position. This isn't how I imagined us finding the treasure.'

Dickpa gave a deep sigh. 'Yes,' he said slowly, passing a trembling hand across his forehead, 'it is the treasure. Do you know what *that* is?' he asked, pointing to an enormous plate of gold on which was engraved a human face from which innumerable rays sprang out in every direction.

'It reminds me of something—a sign representing the sun that I've seen at some time or other,' replied Biggles.

'That's just what it is,' said Dickpa in a low voice, vibrant with ill-suppressed excitement. 'The famous Inca Sun God, made of solid gold. It was known to exist. Well, we shan't take *that* away with us.'

'Why not?' asked Algy quickly.

'Don't you realise how much it weighs?' replied Dickpa with a short laugh.

'No; how much?'

'Tons. Tons and tons. My dear boy, a cubic foot of gold—that is, a piece of gold measuring twelve inches in each direction—weighs about eleven hundredweights—*over half a ton*. If you think you are going to pick all these things up and carry them away with you under your arms, you are sadly mistaken. The Sun God alone contains a good many cubic feet, and so does its sister idol, the Moon God, which I can see over there, although that, according to records, is made of silver.'

Another silence fell in which they feasted their eyes on the most famous treasure in the world, a fabulous El Dorado, which, four hundred years before, would have been part of the ransom of the murdered Inca king but for Pizarro and his Spaniards, who, impatient at the delay in collecting it, committed one of the foulest deeds in history.

The room was one vast treasure-chamber. Round the walls were piled ornaments and utensils of every description, all of fine gold. Immense vases, goblets, dishes, ewers, and articles of all shapes and sizes representing plants, sheaves of corn, birds, animals, and even insects, were stacked in tiers, one above the other. There were hundreds of them, more than they could count. The floor was covered with beautifully wrought gold chests; what they contained they could only surmise. Against them leaned swords, shields, lances, daggers, and even agricultural implements, all of the same precious metal. Cubes of golden tiles were neatly arranged at intervals.

'You must remember,' said Dickpa in a hushed whisper, 'that everything used within the precincts of their temples, even the gardening tools, were of gold. Look at those,' he went on, pointing to a heap of gold sheets, each about the size of the lid of a chest, which seemed to have been roughly handled, for many of them were dented and bent. 'I can guess where those came from; Cuzco, from the temple named, "The Place of Gold." The whole of the lower part of it was sheathed in gold plates held on by cornices of the same metal. Amalgro, Pizarro's brutal lieutenant, got some of it, but most of it defied the efforts of his gold-mad soldiers to remove it, and when they came back the priests had hidden it. And there it lies,' he went on in a voice of unutterable sadness. 'And to think those swinish soldiers actually forced the Inca goldsmiths to melt down their own exquisite work—that part of the treasure upon which they did lay their blood-stained hands—into ingots, so that it could be transported more easily. What vandalism! What should we think of people who plundered our churches and cathedrals and melted down the church plate? Three and a half million pounds' worth of gold they took, to say nothing of precious stones and vast quantities of silver. Never has history before or since provided a picture of such incalculable booty; and to think, in spite of all that, they were not satisfied! All this treasure that we now see would have been theirs, for Atahuallpha had promised to fill a great room in his palace as high as he could reach with gold, but the Spaniards, not taking into account what the transport of such colossal weights over hundreds of miles of mountainous country would mean, slew the Inca and thus defeated their own object.

'But what do I see over there?' he continued excitedly, pointing to what appeared to be several great fringes of coloured cord, like tassels, which hung from heavy gold ornaments.

'*Quipus!* That's what they are, and they are worth more to mankind than all the gold put together, for by this curious means the Incas recorded their history. They had no alphabet or arithmetical symbols, but these served them as well, and they could read them with great speed and accuracy. These might indeed be the national archives, although it was reported that Valverde, Pizarro's villainous head priest, destroyed them all in one vast bonfire, saying they were heretical documents, so much of the history of a wonderful race was obliterated at one fell swoop. Where are you going?' he concluded sharply as Biggles clambered through the hole into the treasure-chamber.

'I don't quite get the hang of this room. Why does the floor slope down like this?' replied Biggles curiously.

The room was, as Biggles had observed, of unusual construction. The floor sloped steeply towards the outside wall, while down the centre ran a deep, wide, polished groove, like a channel.

'What does the channel lead to?' asked Dickpa as Biggles peered cautiously round the corner.

'Nothing,' answered Biggles, stepping back hastily.

'What do you mean—nothing?'

'Nowhere, I should have said. There is a sheer drop at the end of it of umpteen thousand feet into an abyss like the one on the other side of the plateau. It looks like the enormous blow-hole of an old volcano.'

'That's it! I see it all!' cried Dickpa. 'Yes, I am sure this is the solution. You know that after Atahuallpha was murdered the whole population was highly incensed against the Spaniards, and suffered the most dreadful tortures rather than give away the secret hiding-places of the gold they had concealed. They were determined that, whatever happened, the murderers of their god and king—for their ruler was a god as well as a king—should not have such treasure as remained. They must have brought it here and deliberately arranged it so that, should the Spanish Conquistadors find them and carry the place by storm, they could hurl the treasure into space, where it would be lost for ever, rather than allow it to fall into their hands. That was the idea, I am almost certain, and it is one typical of the people.'

Biggles, from inside the room, could see the whole vast panorama of the country below, the forest with the river winding in and out like a great serpent. Almost at his feet was the prairie where they had landed the *Condor*, with the clump of buriti palms, from which

164

they had been driven by the ants, a little to one side. Instinctively his eyes sought and found the stream in which they had left the machine, and a cry of surprise and consternation broke from his lips as he picked it out.

'I thought we covered up the wings and tail with branches!' he cried, staring in amazement at the shining white planes of the amphibian, devoid of covering of any sort.

'So we did,' said Algy quickly.

'Well, they're uncovered now, and I can see things moving—' His voice trailed away to silence.

'Monkeys!' ejaculated Dickpa, who had joined Biggles in the treasure-chamber and taken a small pair of binoculars from his pocket. 'That's what they are, monkeys!'

Biggles groaned aloud. 'Snakes, alligators, ants, and now monkeys. Goodness knows what damage they'll do, quite apart from the fact that the machine as it is stands out like a signpost. If Silas and his crowd come this way, they can't miss it; we'd better see about getting down before they do. And we've got that ghastly bridge to face yet,' he went on, with a shock of realisation of their position, which had momentarily been forgotten in the excitement of finding the treasure. 'I shouldn't go to sleep tonight if we were up here, knowing that I'd got to cross it in the morning. We had better go across right away and get back to the machine as fast as we can, although goodness knows how long it will take us to find a way down from those mountains.' He picked up a heavy tomahawk with a polished copper edge. The handle was wrought of solid gold with an emerald as large as a pigeon's egg in the handle. 'This may come in handy,' he said, swishing it through the air at an imaginary foe.

'And I'll take one of the *quipus*,' said Dickpa. 'I don't suppose I shall get much time for studying it, but I might be able to get an idea of what it is about—I know a little about them.'

Algy was putting a number of the smaller ornaments into his haversack.

'Why burden yourself with those?' asked Biggles in surprise. 'I'm going to land the *Condor* up here as soon as we get back.'

'Land the *Condor* up here on the plateau?'

'Of course; it's the obvious thing to do. There is no point in lugging all this stuff down to the bottom; it would take us weeks, anyway.'

Algy looked at him in open-mouthed surprise for a moment. 'Of course,' he said, 'I didn't think of it; still, there is no harm in taking a few souvenirs in case of accidents. Put a few in your bag, Smyth. A bird in the bag is worth two in the bush,' he went on facetiously, handing the flight-sergeant an exquisitely carved peacock with its tail outspread. 'This would make a nice mascot for the *Condor*,' he added, picking up a metal effigy of a condor in flight. 'Hi! Wait a minute, I'm coming.' His last remark was induced by the fact that Dickpa and Biggles had already started off towards the main doorway, and he hurried after them, throwing furtive glances at the silent figures on the floor as he passed.

At the top of the steps Dickpa paused for a moment to gaze down at the stricken town below. He looked as if he was about to say something, but changed his mind and set off at a steady pace down the steps. The sun was sinking fast over the mountains in such a blaze of glory, as they crossed the plateau, that they would have liked to have stayed and watched it, but twilight was at hand and no time was to be lost if they were to make the passage of the bridge that day.

'I'll give you a lead,' said Biggles calmly as they reached it, and without a moment's hesitation, before they were aware of his intention, he had stepped on to the single tree that formed the bridge, and started across.

He was just about half way when he lurched drunkenly and dropped on all fours. The others, too, were flung to their knees by a shock that seemed to shake the whole plateau. The tremor lasted for perhaps thirty seconds. At the first concussion the lower of the two trees that spanned the chasm had plunged clear into space, turning over and over as it fell, until it looked no longer than a match-stalk. A shrill cry of stark horror burst from Algy's lips as he saw the other one totter and the far end start slipping down the short slope on which it rested. Biggles saw it too, and acted with the lightning-like rapidity that had enabled him to pile up a score of victories in France, and survive.

He raised himself on his toes, crouching low like a runner at the start of a sprint race, and then shot like an arrow across the now sagging beam towards the opposite cliff. He knew he could not reach it when he started, and he was still six feet away from the rock and safety when the bridge collapsed. At the same instant he leapt into the air like a cat. The Express flew out of his left hand and disappeared into the void, while his right, still gripping the tomahawk, flashed over and down and the weapon buried itself like a wedge in a narrow crack on the very lip of the rock. Even then, had the weapon broken, or the blade slipped from its insecure hold, he must have fallen to eternity, but neither happened. For a moment he literally hung over the chasm, and then, in a swift flurry of waving arms and legs, he dragged himself over the edge into safety just as a second tremor, worse than the first, shook the earth. It passed as quickly as before, and all was still; a low mutter like distant thunder rolled echoing away to silence.

Dickpa, who seemed to have aged five years in the last minute of time, looked up with haggard face and sniffed the air. 'Sulphur,' he said succinctly, 'the gas that—' But he did not finish the sentence.

Biggles's face appeared among the rocks on the opposite side of the abyss. 'Brazil,' he jeered savagely, 'Brazil—where the mutts come from.'

'If we'd been five minutes earlier we should all have been across,' observed Algy miserably.

'And if we'd been five minutes later we should all have been up salt creek without a paddle,' returned Biggles philosophically. 'Throw me over a can of corned dickey,* Smyth; you've got the grub. I'm going to fetch the *Condor*—if I can. I don't know where I am, or where it is, and I wouldn't know how to get to it if I did. I'm no mountain goat. I like to see a pair of wings on either side of me before I do the high trapeze act. You ought to see what I've got to face. I'm going off right away while there are still a few minutes of daylight left. Go back to the temple; you can see the *Condor* from there, so you'll be able to see me take off. So long.' With a parting wave he was gone.

* Army slang for corned beef.

Chapter 15

A Perilous Passage

When Biggles had said, 'You ought to see what I've got to face,' he had already taken a shuddering glance at the scene on the opposite side of the rock on which he was isolated. Behind him was the chasm, only thirty feet wide, yet cutting him off as effectually from the others as if it had been three hundred feet. On the other three sides he was confronted by such a stupendous array of peaks that even his iron nerve was shaken to no small extent. He realized, of course, that the pathway across the plateau and the bridge led across the rock on which he stood, and that there should be a continuation of it somewhere, and if there was such a path it would, sooner or later, lead down to more normal terrain. Hunting around, he presently found it in the form of a row of steps, cut like a narrow shelf into the sheer face of the cliff. Where they led he was unable to see, for they wound around a buttress of rock and disappeared. He did not waste time in idle speculation, for he knew that the descent of the awful passage had to be undertaken unless they were all to perish miserably, and delay and contemplation would only make the task more to be dreaded.

He tackled it as he tackled most jobs that were to be feared. He set straight off down the frightful causeway, his right shoulder brushing the face of the cliff and his left in space. He reached the bend, and steadied himself with an effort when he saw that the path continued for at least another fifty yards and again disappeared round a bend. 'Bah! Scores of those Inca fellows must have made this trip regularly, and with loads on their backs, I dare say,' he muttered through his teeth, and, braced with this thought, he continued his way. Curiously enough, the horror of it was already beginning to wear off by the time he reached the next bend, and he realized that it was in the first few awful steps that lay the real danger. He rounded the bend, which brought him facing the direction of the country through which flowed the stream where they had left the *Condor*, but it was now an indistinct world of deep blue and purple shadows falling away in long undulations to the misty horizon. Then, to his unutterable relief, the path widened suddenly and opened out into a small sheltered platform on which, under an overhanging ledge of rock, stood a stone seat. The place had evidently been used in the dim past as a resthouse, for the walls of the cliff were literally covered with carvings, mostly of crude design, representing all sorts of weird creatures that meant nothing to him, but would probably have been familiar to Dickpa could he have seen them. It was now nearly dark. He could see the narrow path winding on again, but he decided it was too risky to attempt in such a light, and settled himself to pass the night as well as he could in the primitive shelter.

Taking everything into consideration, he was fairly successful. He was awakened once by a brief thunderstorm of such violence, and accompanied by such torrential rain, that at one moment he trembled lest the whole side of the cliff, including his precarious perch, be washed away. Fortunately, the overhanging rock protected him; and, remembering that the ledge must have weathered hundreds of similar storms, he crouched a little lower and was soon asleep again.

When he awoke, the sun was shining brightly. He

was rather stiff and sore from the hardness of his couch, and he gazed for a moment uncomprehendingly at the forbidding panorama of towering peaks and frowning precipices before the full significance of his position came back to him with a rush. After a couple of brisk exercises to restore circulation, he looked out at the continuation of the path. As before, it consisted of a flight of steps cut into the rock like a spiral staircase, vanishing round a bend about a hundred yards away and some distance below. Picking up his Inca tomahawk, he set off without further ado.

He was about half way to the bend when a shadow swept across the face of the cliff just in front of him, and, looking round without any particular alarm to ascertain the cause, he saw the largest bird he had ever seen in his life. It was snow white from beak to tail, and he judged it to measure a full twenty feet from wing tip to wing tip. Its cruel curved beak and formidable talons betrayed it to be a bird of prey, and he watched its stately flight in admiration. 'I didn't know there were such things as white eagles,' he mused as he continued his way.*

He had only taken a few steps when a noise of rushing air made him turn quickly with an unpleasant consciousness of danger. The bird was swooping down on him, and he dropped to his knees just as it swept over him, the long curving talons that would have torn his face to ribbons passing within a foot of his head.

---

* Although Biggles did not know it, he was looking at what is probably the rarest bird in the world, the magnificent king condor of the Andes, the existence of which travellers in the Cordillera have reported from time to time. Several attempts have been made to take one dead or alive, but without success. A well-known German naturalist explorer had a very nasty adventure with one. It was named the king condor because ordinary condors seemed subservient to it.

He was on his feet the instant it had passed, hurrying towards the bend, for the narrow shelf to which he clung was no place for an encounter with either bird or beast.

But before he had taken six steps it was clear that the bird had no intention of abandoning its presumed prey, for it soared up in a steep climbing turn and then dropped like a stone towards him, pinions raised, talons projecting viciously below. Biggles grabbed in his pocket for the automatic which he had carried ever since the affair of the Indians, but before he could use it the bird was on him. Instinctively he flung himself down at full length as the bird swept past in a vertical bank at the end of its dive, and the rush of air that followed it nearly blew him from the ledge. He jerked up the automatic, and three fingers of flame leapt from the muzzle. Crack-crack-crack! it spat viciously.

He knew instantly that the bird was hard hit. It faltered in its flight, actually dropping a few feet, and then, recovering itself with an effort, flew to a neighbouring crag, where it settled and then collapsed with outstretched wings. Twice it made a stupendous effort to rise, but failed, and finally, after a convulsive flap of its great wings, it lay still.

'Sorry, old bird, but you asked for it,' muttered Biggles in a tone of sincere regret as he dropped the automatic back into his pocket, for he was genuinely sorry that he had been forced to destroy such a noble-looking creature.

He had nearly reached the bend when a great noise of rushing wings caused him to look up with a start. The air was full of huge, dark-brown birds falling towards him from out of the blue sky. He saw them land, one after the other, with effortless ease on the rock where the white bird lay; then they rose in a cloud and swept towards him with a directness that left no doubt as to their intentions. He waited for no more. As swiftly as he dared he sped along a pathway where, the day before, he would have hesitated to take a single step. He reached the bend with the revengeful winged subjects of the dead king close behind him, knowing that unless some shelter quickly revealed itself he was lost. A single bird he might, and had indeed, vanquished, but a whole flight was beyond his ability to cope with.

He slowed down as he reached the bend lest his impetus should carry him over the brink, and, turning the corner, saw that the path still continued. As he started forward again the sound of gushing water came to his ears from somewhere near at hand, and then he pulled up dead with an involuntary cry of dismay. The path ended abruptly—in mid-air, so to speak. At his feet lay a broad ravine about twenty feet wide; it looked as if the side of the mountain had been split by some mighty convulsion of nature, for he could see the path continuing on its way over the other side. At the bottom of the ravine, forty feet below, a boiling rapid, swollen by the recent rain, raced with headlong, pent-up fury between its narrow rocky confines.

Biggles knew that he was at the end of his tether, for the birds were already swooping to the attack. There was only one thing to do, and he made up his mind quickly. Backing a few yards up the path for the take-off, he sped down the slope and launched himself into space. He knew before he jumped that it was too wide for him, but nevertheless he actually reached the opposite bank; for one awful moment he struggled to maintain his balance, but a rock gave way under his weight and he plunged down into the whirling torrent below.

The icy coldness of the water struck him like a physical blow as he disappeared beneath the surface, but he was up again in a moment, amazed to find he was unhurt. He kept his head and concentrated his efforts on remaining afloat, keeping a watchful eye open for rocks, knowing that it was out of the question for him to attempt to scale the precipitous wall of the canyon. Of the birds he could now see no sign.

From the rate he was travelling he judged the torrent was losing height quickly, and he abandoned himself to it, conserving his strength for a supreme effort in case a break should occur in the side of the canyon sufficient to give him a foothold. He became conscious of a dull booming sound not far away, but from his position at water-level he could see nothing. The noise reminded him of something he had heard before, and even as the word 'Falls' rose to his lips he was hurled outwards and downwards.

Now Biggles, in describing his adventures afterwards to the others, was convinced that he fell a distance of at least a hundred feet, a computation that brought a smile to Algy's face.* Be that as it may, Biggles had a fleeting impression of being pounded to pulp by a tremendous force that surged around him in a world of darkness; a roar like thunder sounded in his ears, and just as he thought his lungs must surely burst he found himself blinking at the sun with his arms resting on something solid. Dazed, gasping like a stranded fish, he wiped his dripping hair from his eyes and saw that he was lying on a shelving sandbank in the middle of

---

* As a matter of fact, this was quite possible. In Samoa and other islands in the South Seas in which high waterfalls occur, the Polynesians think nothing of allowing themselves to be carried over certain falls even higher than this. It is indulged in as a kind of sport rather than a feat demanding nerve and endurance.

a wide, rippling stream. He could see the falls some little distance away churning the water into boiling foam.

At first he was unable to believe that he was still alive, so certain had he been that the cold hand of death had already settled upon him, but he rose gingerly to his feet, and, seeing that the water was fairly shallow, reaching not much higher than his waist, he waded wearily to the nearest bank, where he flung himself down out of sheer exhaustion. In a few minutes his numbed faculties were restored and his frozen limbs beginning to thaw in the sun. A slow smile spread over his face. 'The next time anybody talks to me about going off at the deep end I shall know what they mean,' he mused. 'Well, I suppose I'm still in Brazil.' He rose to his feet and looked around. On his left, and seemingly quite close, towered the perpendicular wall of the plateau. To the right of it were the giant peaks that fell away into a series of foothills, between two of which he now stood. Being in a valley, his field of vision was very restricted, so he set off up the side of the nearest hill to get a better view. When he reached the top and looked down, he could scarcely believe his eyes.

Straight in front of him, and not more than a quarter of a mile away at the foot of the gently sloping hill, was another stream at a lower level, and this he recognized at once as the one up which they had walked to the cave. His eyes swept along it, and came to rest on the *Condor*, standing just as he had left it except that its exposed wings were now shining brightly in the sun.

Delighted with his good fortune, he set off down the hill without delay. 'Dickpa was certainly right about Brazil,' he thought as he pushed his way through creeper-clad bushes and high grass. 'This is the place where you can always reckon on the unexpected happening.

175

Still, this bit of luck wasn't out of its turn.' He struck the stream a trifle below the *Condor*, and he made his way quickly towards it, anxious to learn if any damage had been done by the monkeys. 'I'll get myself a tin of beans before I do anything else,' he thought, suddenly realising that he was famished.

Casually, he opened the door of the cabin. Almost as if to prove what he had just been thinking, the sight that met his eyes was so completely and utterly unexpected that he could only stand and stare in stupefied astonishment.

Upon a cushion, engaged in the prosaic occupation of ladling out the contents of a tin of pork and beans with a spoon, sat a man.

'What's the big idea?' said Biggles coldly, reaching for his automatic and looking the stranger up and down, for he was the most amazing apparition he had ever seen. He was a black man, with curly white hair and a straggling wisp of beard. The tatters of a vest hung over his shoulders, revealing a tattooed battleship on his skinny chest, while in lieu of trousers he wore a strip of old blanket wound about his middle, and this, secured with a liana, served as a sort of kilt. But it was not these things that caught Biggles's eyes and held them fascinated in spite of danger which might threaten. On his feet and legs were a pair of new, beautifully cut officer's field boots, and the whole effect was so incongruous that Biggles could only gape in comical amusement.

'Don't shoot, boss,' answered the man quickly, in English, to his still greater amazement, in answer to his question, nearly choking in his haste to speak with his mouth full of beans. 'I ain't one of them good-fer-nuthin' fellers what's after you—no, sir, that's true sure as God's in heaven. I don't mean no harm, boss—'

176

'Hold hard a minute,' cried Biggles, recovering from his astonishment. 'Are you here alone?'

'Sure, boss.'

'What's your name?'

'Aaron Speakdetruf.'

'What?'

'Honest to God, sir; if my old muther was here she tell you that's truth, sir.'

'Where have you come from?'

'Fust place, way back in Trinidad; second place, way down the river.'

'Trinidad. Is that where you learnt to speak English?'

'That's right.'

'What river are you talking about?'

'Why, this river, sir.'

'What are you doing up here?'

The old negro clasped and unclasped his hands convulsively and his lips twitched. 'Don't take me back,' he begged. 'I—'

'So you're a rubber collector—run away, eh?'

'That's the truth, sir. They told me if I come here and pick rubber pretty soon they take me back home; but I've been here more'n twenty years now, and I ain't had nuthin', don't see nuthin'—'

'And ain't got nuthin',' continued Biggles. 'I see. Well, don't make a song about it. How long have you been in this machine?'

'Just come, sir; found all these monkeys—'

'Did you know we were here?'

'No, sir.'

'But you knew we were about somewhere?' suggested Biggles suspiciously.

'Why, yes, sir; I heard them fellers talking.'

'Talking! What about?'

'Well, 'twas this way. I was going down the river in

177

the old canoe and I met them coming up on the water on the big plane. They say, "Have you seen another plane?" And I say, "No, that's truth. I—" '

'Go on, cut out the rough stuff. What did they do?'

'Why, they beat me, and say they take me back to da Silva.'

'Da Silva?' cried Biggles, staring aghast at the terrible weals on the old man's shoulders, which he had exposed to prove his words.

'Yes, he's my master, sir. I owe him three hundred pounds, he says.'

Biggles, who had heard how the rubber kings controlled their unfortunate labourers by getting them to incur an imaginary debt and then holding them to their jobs without pay, during which the debt invariably grew larger instead of smaller, nodded sympathetically. 'But how did you get here?' he asked.

'I broke away from that camp in the dark night, and I set off anywhere.'

'And you borrowed a pair of boots, I see?'

'Why, yes, sir, I hadn't no shoes of no account. I got back in my ole canoe and went anywhere to get out of those fellers' way. A bad, good-for-nuthin' lot they are! I heard them laughing about you, sir. They say, police all down the river by Manaos and Para all want to hang you for killin' man in the jail at Manaos.'

'Killing, did you say?' cried Biggles, remembering the black gendarme in the jail at Manaos.

'Why, yes, sah. He ain't dead, sir, but they say he is so as they can hang you.'

'I see,' said Biggles slowly, realizing that it was going to be even more difficult to get out of the country than they expected. 'Where are you going now?' he asked.

'I dunno, sir. Seems all the same to me. If I keep going, maybe I'll come to Trinidad sometime.'

'I'm afraid you've got a tidy step in front of you,' observed Biggles. 'Well, I'm afraid I can't take you with me. But give me a hand to haul the machine up on the bank and I'll give you some grub to see you on your way. Come on.'

A quick examination revealed that no damage had been done by the monkeys, who had evidently merely contented themselves with throwing the loose branches off the machine. It proved to be no easy job to move the machine, and Biggles had to start the engine, much to the old man's horror, before the *Condor* finally stood on terra firma. He could not help reflecting on the curious chance that had brought the man his way, for he realized now for the first time that he could never have got the *Condor* out of the stream single-handed.

He taxied out on to the runway where they had landed, and, leaving the engine ticking over, climbed out of the cockpit to give the old man the promised stores. The man, who had evidently never seen so much food before, thanked him with tears in his eyes, and, leaving him to pursue his solitary way, Biggles climbed back into the cockpit with a grunt of satisfaction and opened the throttle.

The *Condor* bumped rather alarmingly over the rough ground, but a light breeze helped her and she was soon in the air, climbing steeply and banking in the direction of the towering cliff upon which Biggles had fixed his eyes. And thus it was that he did not see the tragedy being enacted below, or know how near he had been to disaster as he unhurriedly bid the old rubber tapper goodbye. Later, the others told him.

Simultaneously with his wheels leaving the ground, four men, panting as if they had been running, dashed round the corner of the stream where the *Condor* had stood. The leader, the same pock-marked individual that Biggles had stunned in far-away England, stopped dead with a foul oath.

'Gone,' he said. 'We've missed 'em by a minute. That cursed negro must have told 'em we'd seen the machine and were on our way. There he is now.'

The unfortunate rubber tapper, unaware of their approach, was busy putting his newly found wealth in his canoe, humming an old song as he did so.

'So you found 'em, eh?' snarled Blattner, his lips curled back from his yellow teeth in a bitter snarl.

The black man looked into the bloodshot, evil eyes and read death in them. His face turned a horrible greenish hue. 'No, sir,' he faltered. 'I—'

'You didn't, eh?' snarled Blattner, drawing his revolver.

The man had dropped to his knees. 'Don't shoot, sir,' he implored. 'God's truth, sir—'

A stab of flame spurted from the muzzle of the gun as it roared its leaden message of death.

Two big tears rolled down the old man's cheeks as he slipped forward like a swimmer in deep water.

Again the revolver barked. The man gave a convulsive shudder and then lay still.

Blattner laughed shortly as he pushed the revolver back into its holster. 'That's the only way to serve those swine,' he snarled.

Biggles, three thousand feet above, and some distance away, unaware of the grim fate that had overtaken his recent assistant, and that four pairs of vicious eyes were watching every turn he made, cut off his engine and glided gently towards the smooth surface of the plateau. He knew that he was about to make the most important landing of his life, a landing where the least mistake would have disastrous consequences, not only to himself, but to those he loved best in the world.

Once, over the rim of the cliff, a swirling up-current from the overheated rock brought his heart into his mouth, but he had the *Condor* back on an even keel in a flash, and with hands and eyes as steady as the rock on which he was about to land, he flattened out and dropped lightly on the elevated landing-ground.

When he looked up, a little pale from his ordeal, Dickpa, Algy, and Smyth were running towards him, cheering.

'Easy as A B C,' laughed Algy in relief.

'Easy, was it?' replied Biggles. 'You go and take a running snatch at yourself. What with climbing down crazy staircases built for lunatics, being attacked by mad eagles, falling into rapids, diving over water-falls—'

'And then missing being captured by the skin of your teeth,' broke in Algy, 'you've—'

'*What* by the skin of my teeth?' interrupted Biggles sharply.

'Being captured. You saw Silas and his crowd tearing up the stream, didn't you?'

'Great jumping cats! No, I didn't, and that's a fact,' confessed Biggles. 'What are you talking about?'

'We could see the whole thing from up here, and we nearly went off our heads with excitement. We couldn't make out why on earth you didn't hurry—you seemed to be deliberately taking your time. We were certain they were going to nab you. Who was the other fellow you were with? They've shot him, you know.'

Biggles turned as white as death. 'Shot—him,' he whispered.

'Yes, killed him in cold blood, the devils,' broke in Dickpa.

Biggles sat silent in his cockpit for a moment, and, when he looked up, his face wore a strange expression.

'One day—soon, I hope—I shall kill *them*,' he said stonily.

Chapter 16
Combat Tactics

Over a hurried meal, Biggles briefly described his adventures since his leap for life on the swaying bridge. Dickpa was very intrigued at the description of his battle with the great white bird, which he told him must have been one of the very rare king condors.

The others had little to relate. They had spent a very uncomfortable night on the open plateau, incidentally getting drenched to the skin in the storm that had scared Biggles during his night in the shelter on the cliff. In the morning, not knowing whether he had succeeded in finding a way down, they had repaired to the top of the pyramid, from where they had seen the rubber tapper's discovery of the *Condor*, Biggles's subsequent arrival, and the dramatic sequel. With a smile, Dickpa described how they had all cheered wildly as the *Condor* left the ground under the very noses of the enemy and climbed upwards towards them like a great white gull.

'Well, we aren't out of the woods yet, not by a long way,' observed Biggles. 'One thing is certain; we can't go back the way we came. If we so much as touch our wheels in any civilized part of Brazil—if there is such a place—we shall be slung into jail before we know where we are'; and he repeated the story the rubber tapper had told him of the trumped-up charge against them for 'killing' the prison warder—'the fellow I dotted on the back of the nut with the mooring-spike,' he explained. 'What are we going to do about it?'

'The only solution seems to be to make for Bolivia,' said Dickpa with a worried frown.

'Bolivia! How far away is it?'

'Speaking from memory, I should say we are about two hundred and fifty miles from the Bolivian frontier, and then about another four hundred miles on to La Paz, the capital. But let us look at the map; we have one in the cabin.'

The map was quickly produced, and, spreading it over the lower wing of the *Condor*, they examined their proposed course. The distances Dickpa had given were practically correct, which meant that Bolivia was well within their range, and there was no reason, except possible engine failure, why they should not cover the whole distance in one hop and put themselves beyond the vengeance of their enemies. Dickpa anticipated no trouble with the Bolivian authorities, for he knew many influential people on the Pacific side of the Andes, where he had made several exploring expeditions. They would, of course, have to make an account of their quest and the treasure, and possibly hand over a certain percentage of it to the Bolivian Government, according to the laws of that land, where treasure trove was a by no means infrequent occurrence. What action Brazil would take, when the authorities heard of the discovery of the treasure, they neither knew nor cared. In any case, Dickpa had a permit to search for treasure, granted some years before, and, once back in their own land, it was unlikely that they would be molested, as they undoubtedly would be if they passed through Manaos on their way back. Indeed, Dickpa was quite certain that the fact of treasure being aboard the *Condor* would make the Brazilian authorities still more anxious to intercept them.

Biggles laid a compass course to Lake Titicaca, the

great inland sea of Bolivia, on the shores of which the capital was situated, and where he anticipated no trouble in making a safe landing. Further, it was so large that he could hardly miss it.

'Well, let us see about getting the treasure on board, or as much of it as we can carry,' he suggested. 'Silas & Co. may not suspect that we are not going back the way we came, but there is a good chance that now they know where we are they will try some mischief. Luckily they can't land up here in their flying-boat, but they've got a machine-gun, don't forget, and they might make things a bit hot for us. I don't like the look of the weather, anyway,' he went on, looking around the sky with a speculative eye. 'I have a feeling in my bones that this is a calm before a storm.'

Indeed, the truth of his words was at once apparent to the others, for a curious, uncanny calm had settled over everything. Not a breath of air stirred, and the heat of the stagnant atmosphere was overpowering. The sun no longer shone clearly in a blue sky, but gleamed dully through a yellow haze that shed an unpleasant copper-coloured glow over everything.

'No, I don't like the look of it either,' declared Dickpa. 'I only saw a sky like this once before, and—' His voice trailed away to silence, as if he preferred not to finish the sentence.

'Well, let's get this treasure aboard before we do anything else,' exclaimed Algy, climbing aboard the *Condor* and twirling the self-starter.

The amphibian was taxied carefully across the plateau to the foot of the hill, and they all set off at a good pace up the path towards the summit. They had not reached half way, however, when it became obvious that something was about to happen. The sun became completely obscured behind a red-brown fog that seemed to form in the air above them, and the land-scape became overcast with a dull orange twilight. A steady drizzle of fine grit began to fall; it clogged their mouths and noses and made breathing difficult.

'Stop!' cried Dickpa suddenly.

'Stop nothing!' exclaimed Biggles. 'I haven't come all this way for nothing'; and he broke into a sharp trot. But he did not go far. A long, hollow booming sound filled the air with noise, and then, as if struck with a mighty hammer from below, the ground on which they stood jarred horribly and threw them off their feet. Rocks began to roll down the side of the hill and a cloud of yellow vapour appeared at its crest. Then a wave of choking, sulphurous gas swept over them, half blinding them, and sending them staggering and reeling down the hill.

'Run for it!' croaked Dickpa, whipping out his handkerchief and holding it over his face. He began running down the hill, closely followed by Algy and Smyth.

Biggles stood impotent for a moment; the ground rocked under his feet and a rain of hot cinders began to fall. Panic seized him, and he raced after the others, catching his breath, as, through the gloom he saw a great boulder as large as a house bounce down the hill in great leaps and miss the *Condor* by inches. The earth swayed, quivering to a succession of titanic con-cussions that in places split the side of the hill like piecrust. 'It's the end of the world,' he thought vaguely as he ran. He caught the others, and they reached the machine together, flinging themselves into their places without a word.

'Contact!' came Smyth's voice in a high-pitched scream from his place behind the engine.

Biggles whipped on his goggles, spun the self-starter,

and, as the engine roared, jammed the throttle wide open. Whether he was taking off up-wind or down-wind he neither knew nor cared as the *Condor* lurched across the swaying rock towards the rim of the plateau and staggered into the air like a stricken swan. He had no idea where he was going, but concentrated his attention in trying to keep the *Condor* on an even keel as it roared blindly through the now opaque dust-cloud, torn and twisted by such blasts of hot air that might have been projected from the pit itself.

The next ten minutes were a nightmare of horror that would never be forgotten by any of them. Rocked by bumps of such magnitude that it seemed incredible that the *Condor* could hold together, they wallowed above an inferno that baffled description. Then the fog grew thinner, and at last they could see the forest like a dark green pall below. Biggles drew the stick back gently into his stomach and climbed higher, glancing for the first time at his companion in the cockpit. It was Algy. A feeble grin spread over his face, which was as black as a stoker's from the ash that had adhered to the perspiration on it.

'Nice flying weather for phœnixes,' he yelled, and Biggles, in spite of the seriousness of their position, could not repress a smile.

The air cleared rapidly as they drew farther away from the eruption, for they had no doubt as to the origin of the inferno which now hung over the horizon behind them like a gigantic black mushroom. There would be no more landing on the plateau.

With his eyes on the compass, Biggles was banking gently to lay a westerly course for Bolivia when a shrill yell from Algy made him start up anxiously. A hundred yards away a twin-engined flying-boat was swooping down on them, and the familiar chatter of a machine-gun sounded above the noise of the engine. Heedless of the result it might have on the occupants of the cabin, who could not know what was happening, he flung the *Condor* into a vertical bank that brought him to the side of the other machine away from the gunner; but it instantly swept round in a manner that left no doubt as to the intentions or ability of its pilot.

Biggles knew the crew of the Curtiss were deliberately trying to shoot them down, under the impression that the cabin of the *Condor* contained treasure literally worth a king's ransom. If they succeeded, the flying-boat could return to its base, and its crew afterwards return, on foot, to the crash. His lips parted in the cold, mirthless smile that had become an unconscious habit when he was fighting, and he fixed the pilot of the other machine, now banking steeply on the other side of a narrow circle, with a hostile stare.

It was soon apparent that whoever was flying the Curtiss was no match for the War pilot, at least where manœuvring was concerned; nevertheless, the twin-engined machine was the faster of the two, and that put escape by the simple means of flying away from it out of the question. Biggles could not go on circling indefinitely, for his supply of fuel was already barely sufficient for the long journey ahead. The gunner in the front cockpit of the Curtiss was firing his machine-gun whenever an opportunity offered, and once or twice an ominous *flack, flack, flack*, in his top wing warned Biggles that some of the shots were coming perilously close. He longed for a machine-gun as he had never wanted anything before, for he knew that, thus armed, he could soon have ended the combat. The idea of sending the other machine and its crew crashing down to oblivion did not give him the slightest cause for regret for the cold-blooded murder of the luckless old man was still fresh in his mind. He remembered his automatic, but he knew from experience the futility of such a weapon against an aeroplane, particularly as in order to use it he would have to place himself within the field of fire of his better-armed opponent. 'Something has got to be done about this,' he thought quickly. He beckoned to Algy. 'Get something to throw!' he yelled.

Algy understood at once, and disappeared into the cabin, to return immediately with a two-gallon metal drum of oil, weighing perhaps nearly thirty pounds. He balanced it on his knee and nodded to show that he was ready.

Biggles took a swift glance at his opponent; then he flung the *Condor* on an even keel and dived. Looking back over his shoulder, he saw the other pilot level out and come roaring down on his tail. He waited until it was almost within normal shooting-range, and then he employed the trick invented by the German ace whose name it still bears, and which enabled him to pile up a score of victories before he met a foeman who had brought the manœuvre to a finer state of perfection— the famous Immelmann turn.* Biggles had done it hundreds of times and had brought it to a fine art.

Up, up, roared the *Condor* in an almost vertical zoom, and then, reversing its direction, screamed down on the tail of the Curtiss. He became the pursuer and the other pilot the pursued. His next move was rendered easier by the fact that the other pilot, evidently unaccustomed to combat tactics, appeared to have lost sight of him, for he continued to fly straight on, looking

* This manoeuvre consists of a half roll off the top of a loop thereby quickly reversing the direction of flight. It was named after Max Immelmann, successful German fighter pilot 1914–1916.

quickly to right and left. Finally he looked up over his shoulder and started to turn, but he was too late. The *Condor*, travelling at nearly twice the speed of the other by reason of its dive, swept over the Curtiss, its wheels almost scraping the top plane as it passed. No one but a War pilot would have dared to take such a risk.

As they passed, Algy raised himself up on his seat, the oil drum between his uplifted hands. Then he hurled it down with all his strength. Biggles zoomed.

The drum caught the Curtiss fair and square on the centre section, and the effect was instantaneous. The machine lurched sickeningly, and its top wings folded back like those of a butterfly about to alight. Then it plunged earthward, twisting and turning like a piece of crumpled tissue paper.

Algy, white faced, leaning over the side, saw a wing tear off and float slowly downwards far behind the plunging hull. He shook his head slowly, as if appalled at the deed now it was done, but Biggles was watching him with an expressionless face, his lips compressed into a thin, straight line. Bending over, he shouted, 'Don't worry; they asked for it; now they've got it.' And then, turning back to his compass, pointed the nose of the *Condor* slightly south of west. A few moments later, impelled by some mutual impulse, they looked back. From earth to sky stretched a great blanket of black smoke that hid from human eyes the last stronghold of a mighty empire and the treasure of its murdered king.

Chapter 17
Crashed

Forest—forest—forest. On all sides, reaching to the
horizon, stretched the eternal forest. Would it never
end? For three long hours they had been flying on
their plotted course towards Bolivia, homeward bound.
Biggles had sunk low in his cockpit, utterly weary of
the endless forest that was as monotonous as the open
sea. Once or twice he roused himself slightly and looked
below as they passed over a river that wound its mys-
terious way through the innermost recesses of the
jungle, but no sign of life or habitation could he see.
The immensity of it appalled him, depressed him
beyond measure, possibly because he was by no means
certain, having only a very small scale map for refer-
ence, when they might expect a change of scenery.

The first indication came in the shape of a small
wisp of cloud that appeared above the horizon in front;
it raced towards them, embraced them for a moment
in its clammy grip, and then swept away astern. Two
more appeared, and then a long row of them, advancing
in line like the van of a victorious army. Then came a
long, unbroken belt of cloud.

Biggles frowned and started climbing, not quite certain as to whether it would be safer to fly above the
cloud or below it, but, remembering the stupendous
mountain peaks that lay ahead, he decided it would be
better to get above. Eight thousand, ten thousand, and
then twelve thousand feet ticked up on the altimeter,
and still the ponderous masses of cumulus swept down

threateningly upon them. Fourteen thousand—fifteen thousand—the *Condor* was climbing more slowly now—read the figure under the altimeter* needle. They were clear above the clouds now, flying over a white world of gleaming, unbroken cloud that stretched away to infinity like a perpetual field of snow, as monotonous but more inspiring than the endless vista of forest had been.

Biggles was by no means happy at this new state of affairs. Before, engine failure would have meant a crash, a pancake on the top of the trees below, but he could at least see where he was going and brace himself against the moment of impact. The result would now be the same except that he could see nothing; it would be the difference between collision in broad daylight and collision in pitch darkness. 'Still, why anticipate trouble?' he thought with a shrug of his shoulders. Algy nudged him and pointed. Away to the left, a pale blue pinnacle which seemed to have been built on the cloud itself pointed upwards like a threatening finger a full three thousand feet above them. Behind it were others, some larger, some smaller, some perfectly pointed, others rough and jagged, as if they had been broken off with a mighty hammer.

Biggles knew he was gazing at the advance guards of the Cordillera, the great Andean range that stretches like the backbone of the world down the Pacific seaboard of America. He glanced at his altimeter—fifteen thousand feet. He tilted his nose up slightly and climbed more steeply, wondering how much longer his petrol would hold out under the extravagant expenditure. At eighteen thousand feet he passed the first

---

*Instrument that indicates the height of the aeroplane above sea or ground level.

gigantic sentinel, towering like a cold, grim fortress in some fantastic fairy-tale. Then he passed others, threading his way through them like a mariner in a sea of icebergs, but instead of blue water under his keel it was a rolling ocean of opaque white vapour. It was a scene of desolation and unutterable loneliness, as one imagines the surface of the moon.

As he stared anxiously ahead for a break in the sea of mist, he wondered what lay below. 'More mountains, I suppose,' he mused. He studied his map closely, and decided that they must now be well over Bolivia, but they might as well have been over the North Pole for all the assistance the map gave him.

His engine spluttered and faded out as his main tank ran dry, and he switched over to the gravity tank that contained their last remaining petrol; it would last perhaps half an hour at most. If the clouds still persisted at the end of that time, he would have to come down, whatever lay below. Half an hour! A lot could happen in that time, but the immediate prospect was not alluring. The minutes ticked by and still no sign of a break in the clouds appeared. Biggles's face began to look old and worn. For himself he did not mind; it was the thought of Dickpa, helpless in the cabin, to whom he felt morally responsible for their present predicament.

Another twenty minutes passed, and he bit his lower lip under the strain. Fortunately the peaks were behind him now, but he had no means of knowing if lesser ones thrust their rugged peaks into the cloudbank below. He might strike one the instant he attempted to glide down, in which case the *Condor* and its crew might lie, a broken wreck, undiscovered until the very end of time itself upon some unscalable peak in a world of snow and ice.

His altimeter was useless. He had set it to suit the

altitude of their last landing-place on the prairie, which was fifteen hundred feet above sea-level. The ground below them now might rise to any altitude up to fifteen thousand feet. Vaguely he recalled that the centre of Bolivia was a vast tableland more than ten thousand feet above sea-level, and that Alto de la Paz, the aerodrome of the Bolivian Air Force, was situated at four thousand feet higher than that.

He hoped fervently that the clouds were thin, or, at least, that they did not reach to the ground, so that when the inevitable forced landing became necessary he would be able to 'pancake,' which might not be so disastrous as diving nose first into the ground.

Three minutes left. He glanced hopelessly to the left and then to the right to see if there was any break in that direction.

Thirty feet away from his right wing-tip, and rapidly overhauling him, was another aeroplane. Had it been a whale or an elephant soaring through the air it could not have been more completely paralysing in its effect on him. He did not move; he could only stare, his jaw sagging foolishly.

During the War, and even on the present expedition, he had had many shocks and had learned to be prepared for the unexpected to happen at any time; but this was too much, and for the first time in his life he thought his senses were playing him false. For a moment he thought it might be his own shadow on an invisible cloud, or some sort of miraculous mirage such as occurs in the desert, but he quickly discarded the idea as impossible as he recognized the machine as a three-engined Junkers. The pilot was beckoning frantically to him, obviously trying to convey some signal, which he presently interpreted to mean that he was to follow him. With his brain still reeling from the shock, he instinctively, moved the joystick in the necessary direction, but with a choking splutter the engine cut out dead, and an instant later the *Condor* was enveloped in a sea of swirling grey mist.

The next few minutes, during which it gradually grew darker as they sank into the cold heart of the cloud, were a nightmare that haunted both pilots for many a day. Biggles held the stick back until the *Condor* was almost stalling along, the speed indicator quivering on the fifty-five miles an hour mark, which, although comparatively slow, was a speed sufficient to dash them all to eternity should they strike a cliff. The fog became still more dense until it was impossible to see the wing-tips, and he began to grow dizzy from the strain of trying to keep the machine on an even keel, with no landmark to guide him.

Nine thousand, eight thousand, seven thousand — the altimeter needle crept slowly down the dial. Where was the ground? Was it only fifty feet below? He did not know, and had no means of finding out. Algy drew his knees up to his chin and buried his face in his arms, a posture frequently adopted by many pilots and observers when they knew a crash is inevitable, the idea being that a human body, rolled up into the form of a ball as far as possible, is less likely to be broken or trapped in the wreckage.

Six thousand five hundred! Biggles bit his lip until it showed white under the pressure; the strain was becoming unbearable. Then, suddenly, the mist cleared slightly as they emerged into a world of twilight, lashed by the soaking downpour of a tropical rainstorm. The ground loomed darkly two hundred feet below.

A swift penetrating glance and he knew they were lost. They were over forest — not the flat forest of the Amazon basin, but great tree-clad slopes. In one place only was the ground anything like level, but even that was broken by tangled patches of shrub and loose boulders. He side-slipped steeply towards it, for it represented their best chance—not to save the machine, for that was out of the question, but their lives. In that critical moment the pilot's skill and nerve did not desert him. He zigzagged, under perfect control, between several great trees that rose a full hundred feet into the air, missing them by inches, levelled out, and then, as the machine sank towards the earth, pulled the stick back into his stomach. The wheels hit a boulder with a bump that shot the machine twenty feet into the air again. The *Condor* wallowed sickeningly as she lost flying speed and plunged earthwards again. The wing-tip struck a rock, swinging the machine round at right-angles, and then, with a crash of breaking timber and ripping fabric, thrust itself far into a clump of bushes and came to a standstill.

For a moment all was silent except for the spatter of the teeming rain. Then, 'Well, we're still alive, anyway,' came Dickpa's voice from within the cabin.

'We are, but we've no right to be,' replied Biggles with a nervous, high-pitched laugh. 'Great jumping-cats, if this is civil flying, give me war flying every time—it's child's play compared with this. Well, it looks as if the poor old *Condor*'s made her last flip; pity we couldn't have got her back after all she's been through.'

He eyed the wreckage of the once trim amphibian sadly. One wing-tip had been completely torn off where it had struck the rock; the undercarriage was a tangled mass of struts, torn tyres, and bent wheels, while the fabric on the wings was ripped and torn in many places. 'It isn't so bad as one might expect,' he observed, casting a professional eye over the damage. 'What do you think about it, Smyth?'

'No, it isn't,' agreed the old flight-sergeant. 'The main members are still intact, which is the most important thing. She'll never fly out of *this* place, of course, even if we were able to repair her, but I should say that if we were in a civilized country it would be possible to get her repaired.'

'Well, we're not, and, if appearances are anything to go by, we are in just about the most uncivilized country in the world,' observed Algy gloomily.

'I wonder where we are,' muttered Dickpa. 'One thing is certain, we can't do anything while this downpour lasts; let's all get into the cabin; we might as well make ourselves as comfortable as possible.'

The awkward angle at which the hull had come to rest was hardly comfortable, yet it did at least protect them from the drenching rain, which added to the general depression occasioned by the loss of the machine.

'All the same, it might have been a lot worse, believe me,' exclaimed Biggles optimistically as they foraged among their rapidly dwindling provisions. 'By the way, I had a most extraordinary experience just as we dropped into the cloud. Do you know, I saw another machine flying alongside us—at least, I thought I did, but now I'm not so sure about it.'

'Another machine!' cried Dickpa incredulously.

'Wait a minute, why not?' broke in Algy in a flash of inspiration. 'What sort of a machine was it?'

'A three-engined Junkers.'

'And we're in Bolivia, aren't we?'

'We must be well over the border,' declared Dickpa. 'Then it might have been one of the machines of the Lloyd Aero Boliviana; they've got an air line here, you

know; it connects the principal towns in Bolivia. I
remember reading about it, and seeing some pictures
of their machines—yes, they were Junkers, too.'

'Well, that must be the answer,' rejoined Biggles. 'It
was a tri-motor Junkers, I saw, I'm quite sure about
that.'

'What a bit of luck,' went on Algy, spreading some
jam over a biscuit. 'If the pilot saw us, he'll be certain
to come and look for the crash when he finds we haven't
arrived anywhere—or he will as soon as the weather
clears.'

'That puts a different complexion on things,' smiled
Dickpa. 'I was not so worried about the loss of the
machine, which has really served its purpose now, as
I was about the possibility of finding we were down in
the Yungas country somewhere. That's a terrible place,
rotten with fever. So it looks as if all we can do is to
wait for morning and see what it brings forth.'

Chapter 18
Conclusion

They awoke the following morning to find the land-scape shrouded in dense white fog. It was cold, too, and Dickpa insisted on them all taking a big dose of quinine. 'We shall all find ourselves down with fever if we don't take care,' he prophesied, as he stamped briskly up and down. 'This is proper fever weather. I wish this confounded fog would lift; we can't do a thing while it lasts; but the sun will soon shift it when it gets a bit higher.'

Smyth soon had a brisk fire burning, over which they crouched while they consumed hot coffee and biscuits.

'What is it, Dickpa—are you trying to read the future?' asked Biggles, noticing that his uncle was star-ing into the fire with a curious expression on his face.

'No-o, I was looking at that stone,' replied Dickpa slowly, pointing to a piece of rock that had been used to balance the kettle over the fire.

'Why, what's wrong with it?' enquired Biggles curi-ously.

'Nothing's wrong with it,' answered Dickpa quickly. 'Take a look at it yourself, though. Notice anything?'

The others turned puzzled eyes on the side of the rock nearest the fire at which Dickpa was pointing. Across it ran several uneven, pale grey lines; the effect was not unlike a stone across which a snail had crawled, leaving a thin shining trail. A tiny bead was oozing down it.

Dickpa reached out and picked up a piece of rock

that lay near by. He balanced it for a moment in the palm of his hand, as if trying to judge its weight, and then, producing a small magnifying-glass from his pocket, he examined it closely. 'There's metal in this,' he announced.

'What—gold?' cried Algy.

'No, not gold, I'm afraid,' answered Dickpa, 'but I should say it is silver. Look! You can see traces of it with the naked eye; metal has to exist in fairly large quantities before you can do that. If it is silver, it looks as if we've struck something that might make us well off, if not rich, after all. There must be a vein of it somewhere handy.' He walked towards a sharp rise in the ground that loomed darkly in the fog. In one place there had recently been a minor landslide, caused possibly by the action of the recent heavy rains, for a mass of torn and tangled vegetation lay at the foot, exposing the bare face of the hill. 'There it is!' he cried instantly, pointing to a broad diagonal line that stood out boldly on the face of the rock. 'By Jove, what an amazing coincidence that we should literally crash on to the very place that a prospector might spend his life looking for. Not a word about this to anybody. I'll put a few pieces in my case and get it assayed as soon as we reach civilization,' he told the others, who were listening open-mouthed.

'It doesn't look as if we're likely to tell anyone in this place, so I shouldn't worry on that score,' observed Biggles, grinning. 'Hooray, here comes the sun!'

The others joined him in a cheer as the grey fog lifted suddenly, as if it had been drawn up by an invisible hand. It grew lighter rapidly; the mist became a blinding white glare, and then the sun broke through and the moisture-drenched landscape lay before them. They realised instantly and for the first time how lucky they had been in the forced landing. To the east the ground fell away quickly, with the forest increasing in density at the lower altitudes, until at last it stretched in an unbroken jungle to the distant horizon. On the other three sides, steep hills, partly covered with patches of stunted cedar-trees, rose from the narrow shelf on which they had crashed and prevented them from seeing what lay beyond.

'Luck's a funny thing, isn't it?' soliloquized Biggles philosophically. 'I've seen a fellow spin into a tree from a thousand feet and get away with a broken nose; and another fellow touches his wheels on a sunken road as he comes in to land, somersaults, and breaks his neck. If we'd come down one minute earlier or later we must have gone nose first into the side of a hill or into the thick forest. We've had some luck on this show, taking it all round—Hello, here she comes!' he went on excitedly, pointing to the sky, whence came the roar of a high-powered aeroplane. 'It's the Junkers—looking for us, too, by the way he's circling. Chuck some green stuff on to the fire so that he'll see the smoke.' As he spoke he tore up an armful of brushwood and flung it on to the fire; the others did the same, and a tall column of thick white smoke rose like a pillar into the air.

As he had prophesied, the pilot of the air liner saw it almost at once, and, throttling back his engines, dived steeply in their direction. The stranded airmen ran out into the open and waved caps, coats, and anything they could lay hands on.

'Ghr-r-r-r-r-r-r-r—' roared the big plane as it swept low over them, and they could see curious faces staring down from the cabin windows.

'All right, stand fast,' called Biggles; 'he's seen us. I don't know what he'll do, though—he's not likely to try and land here. Hullo, here he comes again.'

Once more the Junkers roared past them, at little more than stalling speed this time, and, as it passed, an arm emerged and a white object fell like a stone. The plane circled in a steep bank, dipped its wings, and then headed westward.

'What is it?' asked Dickpa of Algy, who had retrieved the message, for they had no doubt as to the nature of the object that had been thrown down to them.

Algy snorted. 'You'd better read it, I can't,' he said, passing a small piece of paper which had been enclosed in a cigarette-case rolled up in a handkerchief.

'*Descanso*,' read Dickpa. 'That means "rest"—they mean we are to wait where we are, I suppose. It looks as if they are going to send assistance.'

'In that case I'll finish my breakfast,' observed Biggles.

They had less time to wait than they expected, for in rather less than two hours a party of men dressed in the blue overalls of mechanics appeared from a ravine in the hills to the west and hurried towards them, shouting, as they came, in a language which Dickpa told the others was Spanish, and to which he replied readily as they arrived on the scene.

The newcomers talked volubly as they examined the wrecked *Condor* with the greatest interest, shaking their heads and gesticulating wildly. Biggles, unable to understand a word of what was being said, sat on a rock and watched the performance with bored impatience.

'Hi, what is it all about, Dickpa,' he called at length. 'Don't keep all the news to yourself.'

'We were luckier than we knew,' Dickpa told him. 'We have crashed quite close to Cochabamba, right on the direct air route between Santa Cruz and Cochabamba. In fact, they say we actually flew right over

Santa Cruz aerodrome yesterday afternoon and they sent a machine up to see who the dickens it was.'

'That must have been the machine I saw,' declared Biggles.

'It was. The pilot saw you disappear into the fog and thought that was the end of you. He went back to Santa Cruz then—or, rather, they called him back by directional wireless. He had to fly some passengers and mails to Cochabamba this morning, so he kept a look-out for us, and, as you know, he spotted us. He reported our position by wireless to Cochabamba, and the traffic manager sent out this party to see what could be done.'

'Then we shall have to walk to Cockadoodle, or whatever you call the place?' said Biggles.

'*Cochabamba.*'

'That's it. We'll make loads of the most important stuff, but I suppose we shall have to leave the rest behind. I'm taking my gold tomahawk, anyway. What about the machine?'

'I've spoken to them about that. The chief mechanic says they can dismantle it and take it back in pieces to their workshops, where he thinks it could be repaired. Alternatively, they'll ship the pieces back to England if we want them to.'

'I would suggest leaving it for them to repair,' returned Biggles, thinking deeply. 'If they can put her in order again and can find room for her in a hangar, well, she would be on the spot ready for us if we came back at any time. If we didn't, then you could probably sell her; she's bound to be worth something, as there is nothing wrong with the engine.'

'Come back again, did you say?' cried Dickpa. 'Haven't you had enough thrills yet?'

Biggles grinned sheepishly. 'Enough for a bit,' he confessed, 'but it just struck me that if we got bored at

203

any time we might fly back and see if the eruption left anything of Ata—'

'Shh!' warned Dickpa. 'One of them might understand English and I haven't told them the real object of our quest, naturally. We had better forget about that for the time being. All right, then I'll tell them to take the pieces to Cochabamba as soon as they can. They are going back now to report, so we had better go with them, and then we'll go on to La Paz. We might as well fly—that will be the quickest way—but I shall have to charter a special machine, because there isn't a regular service. It isn't far—about a hundred and thirty miles or so, I believe. We'll make up loads of all the stuff we want to take; these fellows have nothing to carry, so they'll help us.'

The baggage was quickly collected from the cabin of the wrecked machine, the gold ornaments which represented the fruits of the expedition being kept together in a special bag, which was entrusted to Smyth. As they examined these, they found them to be more numerous than they thought, and Dickpa pronounced himself to be more than satisfied with the result. In addition to Biggles's tomahawk, with its huge emerald, which alone was worth an enormous sum, there was an exquisitely carved peacock with jewelled eyes, and a condor, both of which were of fine gold and weighed several pounds. Algy and Smyth had put a few ornaments in their haversacks before leaving the treasure-chamber, and these included, on Algy's part, two small gold llamas, a priest holding a rod with a good-sized ruby in the end, a sheaf of corn, and three other small gold ornaments of no particular form but of beautiful workmanship.

Smyth's bag revealed a pair of long, jewelled earrings, an effigy of a warrior with sword raised, a chain, or necklace of gold filigree work, with pearls, five small animals and birds, and a fine goblet. The latter had been badly dented in the crash, but not beyond a good goldsmith's ability to repair.

As Dickpa pointed out as they trudged along behind the Bolivians, he was not really very interested in the intrinsic value of what they had found. Each piece was of untold wealth from a historical point of view, and the *quipus* he had taken alone compensated him for the trouble and expense of the quest. Indeed, he declared himself ready to make another trip at any time for even less results.

A walk of two hours brought them to the aerodrome of Cochabamba, where, after giving an account of their adventure, or as much of it as they deemed wise, and making final arrangements for the salvage and storing of the *Condor*, they embarked in a specially chartered machine for La Paz, the capital of Bolivia. Through the cabin windows they saw, not without a tinge of regret, the passing of the forest in which they had had so many stirring adventures.

A few formalities had to be arranged with the authorities, and here Dickpa's knowledge and experience of the country stood them in good stead. A mining concession was taken out in respect of the vein of silver they had discovered and the matter left in the hands of a reliable agent until such time as the quality of the ore could be determined.

A week later they sailed from the port of Mollendo, homeward bound, and as they leaned against the rail watching the towering peaks of the Andes drop astern, a queer smile spread over Dickpa's face.

'Well, boys,' he said slowly, 'what do you think of South America now?'

'As a cure for boredom it should take first prize, and

I've a feeling in my bones that I shall see it again,' observed Biggles quietly.

'Me too,' declared Algy.

'Then you'll need a mechanic, sir,' murmured Smyth softly.